GUINEA DOG 3

Other Works by Patrick Jennings You Might Enjoy

Odd, Weird & Little

Guinea Dog 2

My Homework Ate My Homework

Invasion of the Dognappers

Lucky Cap

Guinea Dog

Short Story

A Very Merry Guinea Dog (digital only)

GUINEA DOG 3

EGMONT
USA
NEW YORK

Patrick Jennings

For Regina Griffin, Eagle-eyed, Lionhearted Queen of Editorship

EGMONT

We bring stories to life

First published by Egmont USA, 2014
443 Park Avenue South, Suite 806
New York, NY 10016

1 3 5 7 9 8 6 4 2

www.egmontusa.com
www.patrickjennings.com

Library of Congress Cataloging-in-Publication Data

Jennings, Patrick.
Guinea dog 3 / Patrick Jennings.
pages cm
Summary: When Pedro admits that he has a paralyzing fear of water, his friends try to cheer him
up with a pet. Only this one won't leave the water! The third installment of the Guinea Dog series.
ISBN 978-1-60684-554-7 (hardcover) — ISBN 978-1-60684-555-4 (eBook)
[1. Guinea pigs—Fiction. 2. Family life—Fiction. 3. Camping—Fiction. 4. Fear—Fiction.]
I. Title. II. Title: Guinea dog three.
PZ7.J4298715Gug 2014
[Fic]—dc23
2013044867

Printed in the United States of America

Contents

1. I need a vacation. 1
2. My mom invited my worst friend again. 7
3. My dad needs a vacation. 12
4. I thought caravans had camels. 18
5. We don't rest in the rest area. 23
6. White Crappie Lake isn't as bad as it sounds. 29
7. "Coatimundi!" 34
8. I have no idea how to give CPR to a guinea pig. 39
9. Pablo doesn't swim. 45
10. Dad doesn't like *hot* dogs, either. 49
11. Dmitri can't keep the sixth one down. 56

12. Solar energy from the moon. **62**

13. Adults, rodent cages, and a girl in a long skirt. **70**

14. The only way to get one off you is to chop off its head. **76**

15. Lurena the Pest. **81**

16. 2 guys + 2 dogs + 1 skiff = fun × 5 trillion. **86**

17. Tom Sawyer dries off in the gigantic RV. **90**

18. Mosquitoitis. **95**

19. We couldn't find the mini-mall pet paradise. **99**

20. Truckers must get lonely on the wide-open road. **103**

21. Why does Mom think a guinea pig is the answer to everything? **109**

22. "Cowamundi!" **114**

23. Most fireflies fly higher than guinea dogs. **121**

24. Who knew Fido was a bloodhound? **128**

25. Guinea turtle? **134**

26. Empty speed ahead.　**139**

27. Heroic, sure, but not smart.　**143**

28. Dog-paddling isn't just for dogs.　**148**

29. The guinea dog chased the guinea
squirrel up a tree.　**154**

30. Man eats dog.　**159**

1. I need a vacation.

All the fuss at school about my guinea dog, Fido, has worn me down. Everyone kept bugging me to see the guinea pig that acted like a dog, or asking me where to get one, or otherwise being very annoying. It was exhausting.

Fortunately, next week, my family is heading to White Crappie Lake for our annual camping trip. (The lake is filled with white crappies, which is a kind of fish, but, even so, I'm sure they could have come up with a better name.) My best friend, Murphy, and his family are coming, too. They go with us every year. It's a summer vacation tradition that traces back to when we were in kindergarten together. We've been friends that long. Murphy's the greatest guy in the whole world. I'm lucky he's my best friend and I'm his, because everybody loves Murphy—including Dmitri.

My worst friend, Dmitri, has been trying to replace me as Murph's best friend ever since he moved to Rustbury last summer. He's always trying to impress Murph with all the cool devices and clothes and stuff his rich parents buy him. But Murph doesn't care about that kind of stuff. He would have accepted Dmitri as a friend anyway. His motto is "The more the merrier!"

Murph and I always have so much fun at the lake. We swim, dive off the floating pier, jump off the tire swing, go boating, explore the woods, and just, you know, hang out, without any interruptions, from school or from Dmitri.

This will be Fido's first trip to the lake, of course. I mean, I've only had her a little while. Murph loves her, and so does his dog, Buddy, who is probably the greatest dog in the whole world. Murph says Fido's the greatest guinea pig in the whole world. He's the one who came up with the idea of calling her a "guinea dog."

Right now I'm busy packing for the trip, but

it's hard because every time I put something in my duffel bag, Fido dives in and drags it out and wants to play Tug-of-War. Or she hides it under my bed. Or she tries to chew it to pieces. She chews a lot of things to pieces, and not just my stuff, but Mom's and Dad's, too. Mom laughs it off. Dad doesn't. One of the bazillion reasons he won't let me get a dog is that dogs chew things up.

"Put that down," I say to Fido. "I'm not interested in playing Tug-of-War with my underwear."

She holds on and growls. She wants to play.

So do I. I hate packing.

I dig under my bed and find a sock that hasn't been chewed to bits. She drops my underwear and dives under the bed, snatching the sock before I can get to it, then races in circles around the room, the dirty sock in her tiny teeth.

"Hey, you," I say, pretending I'm sore at her. "Bring that here. Fido, here!"

This is an order, and she obeys. She's a good

dog that way. She inches toward me with her butt up in the air, growling in her deep voice, which is about as deep as a mouse's.

"Come on," I say. "Give it here. Give it. Fido? Fido? Give me the sock."

She hunkers down, her ears low.

I lunge forward and grab the other end of the sock. She tightens her grip, digs her claws into the carpet, and starts shaking her head back and forth. We both tug. I have to pretend she might actually jerk the sock out of my hand, which is impossible. If I wanted to, I could lift it up in the air with her dangling from it by her teeth.

A knuckle knocks on my door.

"Rufus?" my mom says, poking her head inside. "Can I come in?"

"Can't you see I'm busy?" I ask.

"I can," she says, with a that's-so-cute smile. "I just thought I'd tell you the exciting news."

"Exciting?" I ask.

Mom's idea of exciting and mine are pretty different.

"I just got off the phone," she sings. Singing

her words is a sign she's about to break some bad news. This is not looking good.

"Oh?" I ask.

Fido keeps growling and tugging.

"Another fa-mi-ly will be joining us on the tri-ip!" Mom sings.

"What family? And just say it, Mom. Don't sing it."

She sucks in her bottom lip and makes her oh-you're-getting-so-smart-and-grown-up face.

"*Who*, Mom?" I demand. "*Who* is coming with us?"

She opens her eyes and mouth wide in fake anticipation, as if she were building suspense. If I had a drum set, I'd give her a drum roll, but Dad says I can get a drum set when I'm grown up and living on my own, not before.

"*Mom*," I say. I wonder if she's read that book I've seen on her bookshelf, *How to Talk So Kids Will Listen, and Listen So Kids Will Talk*. If she did, she didn't learn anything.

She steps inside the room. "I thought it'd be fun," she says, "to have another family join us on our White Crappie trip this year, so I invited . . ." She pauses for effect.

I scream at her with my eyes: *Go on!*

"I invited Dmitri and his family!"

I let go of the sock, and Fido rolls away like a coconut.

2. My mom invited my worst friend again.

I'm both shocked and unsurprised. How is that possible?

Leave it to Mom. After all, this is the woman who invited not only Dmitri, but also his vicious chow, Mars, to my last birthday party. She also invited Lurena, the annoying, rodent-crazy, old-fashioned-clothes-crazy, *crazy*-crazy girl who has been following me around ever since I got Fido.

Mom has been pressuring me to be friends with Lurena ever since they met. Can't Mom see she's a girl? A *weird* girl? Does she not remember that Lurena once asked her parents for a pet *squirrel*? (Which she got, in a way, when Fido gave birth to a guinea pup that acted like a squirrel.)

Yeah, I gave her Fido's baby. It just made sense. The weird thing about it, though, is that it made us sort of related. That doesn't mean we're friends, of course. Mom hasn't succeeded in making that happen, but I'm sure she hasn't given up.

Inviting Lurena and Dmitri to my birthday party was clueless, but inviting Dmitri on our summer trip to the lake goes beyond normal, everyday parental cluelessness. I'm furious.

"Are you *nuts*?" I yell. I know a person shouldn't yell at his mom, and deep down, I feel bad about it, but on the surface, where my mouth is, I'm too furious to stop myself. "You invited *Dmitri*? Are you *nuts*?"

Fido yelps and runs under my bed.

Mom seems genuinely surprised that I'm angry. Which, again, is shocking but unsurprising.

"How could you?" I'm still yelling. I'm also puffing hard through my nose, like a bull in a bullfight, or like Dad when I put recyclables in the regular garbage. "Don't you remember how mean Dmitri was at my birthday party?

Don't you know by now that I can't *stand* him?"

"I just thought . . . ," she starts to say.

"No, you didn't! You didn't *think*. You *couldn't* have!"

"You know, I'm going to come back when you're ready to talk about this respectfully . . ."

"Respect? You want to talk about *respect*? I'll talk about respect! Respect—"

"I'll come back," she interrupts, and edges toward the door. "Try to calm down. You're scaring Fido."

I growl. Not like a guinea dog. Like a lion. I'm a bull and a lion combined. I'm a savage lionotaur on a rampage. Look out, Mom.

She slips out, but before she pulls the door shut, she stops to flash a toothy, hopeful smile, like I'm an angry guard dog and she just stepped over the line into my territory. Then she says, "I kind of invited Lurena's family, too." And closes the door.

"WHAT?" I scream. The lionotaur pounces at the door, snorting, fangs bared. I pull it open with my claws. Mom is fleeing down the hall.

"I won't go!" I scream. "I won't! I'm not

going! I'm staying here! You hear me? *I'm not going!* I'll stay here alone! Just me and Fido!"

I hear whimpering from under the bed, and the fire of my anger fades, doused by guilt. I'm scaring the poop out of my guinea dog.

I kneel down and peek under the bed. She's there, curled up in the farthest corner, shivering.

"Did you hear that?" I whisper. "Mom invited Dmitri and Mars."

She shivers harder. She doesn't like them any more than I do.

"Unbelievable, right? She also invited Lurena."

Fido stops shivering. She wags her tail— well, she wags the spot where a tail would be if she had one. She likes Lurena okay, but, to her, Lurena means Queen Girlisaur, Fido's daughter.

I sit down on the carpet. This is over. Mom wins. Lurena and her rodents, and Dmitri and his giant puffball are coming on the trip. On top of that, I realize I have to apologize to Mom for yelling at her.

I hope one day I have kids. I'll let them have whatever pets they want, and whatever friends they want. I won't push anything they don't want on them, or deny them anything they do want.

Except cats, of course. I won't live with a cat. That's a no-brainer.

Fido scoots out from under the bed and jumps up into my lap. She gets up on her hind legs and looks me straight in the eye.

"Yeah," I say. "Queen Girly is coming on the trip."

She starts licking my face as if it were an ice-cream cone.

3. My dad needs a vacation.

But he doesn't like vacations. Especially camping trips. Does he have a single reason for this? No. He has a million reasons:

- His study is at home. (He works at home.)
- His kitchen is at home. (He does all the cooking.)
- His washing machine and dryer are at home. (He does the laundry.)
- His bed is at home.
- His bathroom is at home.
- He doesn't like driving.
- He definitely doesn't like driving far from home.
- He doesn't like sleeping in a crowded

pop-up camper without a decent kitchen, washing machine, dryer, or study.

- He doesn't like sleeping on a camper mattress.
- He doesn't like sharing a camper with a guinea pig.
- He doesn't like the way guinea pigs smell.
- He's not crazy about the way I smell.
- He says frogs and crickets keep him up all night.
- He hates mosquitoes.
- He despises ticks.
- He doesn't like cooking over an open fire.
- He doesn't like campout food, not even marshmallows.
- He doesn't like campfires.
- He doesn't like campfire smoke.
- He doesn't like that kids and dogs run around all the time, making lots of noise and going to the bathroom outside.
- He doesn't like swimming in lakes because they're filled with fish, snakes, turtles, dogs, and screaming, splashing kids.
- He doesn't like swimming in lakes because

fish, snakes, turtles, dogs, and kids go to the bathroom in lakes.

- He doesn't like camping in the summer because it's hot and humid, and there's no air-conditioning or even electric fans.
- There's also no Wi-Fi.
- There is nowhere to get a decent cappuccino.
- Porta-Potties.

He's been packing the car and the camper all day. He's like that. Everything has to go in just so. If Dad played video games (he doesn't), he'd love Tetris.

He's sweaty and grouchy, and I'd love to stay miles away from him, but Fido thinks that Dad's putting the stuff into the car and the camper, then taking the stuff out of the car and the camper is a game, so she keeps jumping into the car or the camper, then jumping out of the car or the camper with something Dad just packed. I have to hang around to make sure Dad doesn't kill her.

"Will you get this blasted creature out of

my way?" Dad says, without parting his teeth.

"I'm trying," I say.

"Why don't you put a leash on her and take her for a walk?"

"Okay," I say.

I get Fido's leash—it's actually a leash for a ferret—and click it on to her ferret collar.

"Come on, girl. Let's go for a walk."

Fido digs in. She doesn't want to walk. She wants to play with Dad.

I tug on the leash. She tugs back.

"She doesn't want to go," I say to Dad.

He gives me the Stony Stare. "Well, show her who is the boss."

"Right. Come *on*, Fido," I say, jerking the leash a little harder. She chokes.

I turn to Dad. "She—"

"Get her out of here!"

"Check," I say—forgetting that saying this annoys him—and bend down and scoop up Fido.

She whines.

"Sorry, girl, but Dad needs some space. How about a little Frisbee?"

She immediately stops whining and starts panting.

"Let's go out back," I say, and carry her around to the backyard.

The Frisbee is lying in the grass. It has tons of tiny teeth marks in it. I unhook Fido's leash and toss the disc into the air. She runs it down, makes a sweet aerial catch, then drags it back to me.

"Good one," I say, and scratch her on the head. She pants. She wants me to throw it again.

I do, again and again, and she catches it each time and brings it back. She could do this all day, but I get tired of it and sit down on the grass. She runs over to me and hops up and down. She doesn't want me to quit. Where does she get all this energy?

Funny, that's what my mom always says about me.

"We're going to have some vacation," I say to her. "With Dmitri. And Lurena. And Dad."

I roll my eyes.

"At least Murphy will be coming."

Fido starts whining and clawing at my shirt. She looks up at me with her big puppy eyes and cocks her head to the side. It's hard to refuse.

"Okay," I say, standing up.

I toss the Frisbee for the fiftieth time, and she darts after it.

I'm glad she'll be coming, too.

4. I thought caravans had camels.

Not necessarily. Sometimes a caravan is just cars traveling together.

Our caravan (it's Dad's word, of course) is Mom's hybrid pulling our pop-up camper; Murph's dad's Jeep pulling the wooden teardrop camper Murph's dad built himself; Dmitri's parents' RV that's bigger than a school bus, which is pulling one of their SUVs; and Lurena's parents' hybrid, which isn't pulling anything. They have their dome tent packed in the hatch.

"Did you know they used a camel for Chewbacca's voice?" Murph asks.

He's riding with us on the way to the lake, and I'm riding with his family on the way back.

I'm a firm believer in saving the best for last. Murph's dad is very cool. Not only does he own a Jeep and build cool things like campers, but he doesn't ever think about recycling or vocabulary. He's a regular, dog-loving dad. Unlike mine.

Mine said Murph's perfect dog, Buddy, couldn't ride with us in our car.

"Who or what is Chewbacca?" Dad asks, which is a perfect example of how weird he is.

"He's a character in *Star Wars*, Art," Murph politely explains. Murph's nice to everyone, even dog-hating dads who dislike camping and don't know anything about *Star Wars*. "He's a Wookiee, which is this alien species that are really tall and furry but act pretty much like us. He has arms and legs, and sits and even operates a spaceship, but his face looks like a Maltese."

"Does he chew tobacco?" Dad asks.

Murph and I look at each other. Then Murph says with a laugh, "I never thought about that! You're so smart, Art!"

I hadn't thought of it, either. *Chewbacca* has

always just been the character's name, like my name is Rufus. It never meant anything more than that. I'm sort of proud that my dad came up with the connection.

I'm also impressed that Murph compared Chewbacca to a Maltese. It's true. Chewbacca does have a face like a lapdog. Plus he knows that they used a camel for his voice. I wish I had something smart to say.

"Did you know that camels don't actually spit at you?" Murph asks before I can come up with anything. "They vomit at you."

My mom peeks in her rearview mirror at us. She's driving. Dad's riding shotgun. "Really? That's so gross."

Murph may be a smart guy, but that doesn't mean you should trust the things he says. He not only loves fooling you with made-up facts, but he also fools you by saying things that sound crazy so that you accuse him of making it up, when actually they're totally true. Like when he claimed there were frogs that had claws and hair skirts. I didn't believe him. I should have.

"Spitting is shooting saliva from your mouth," Murph says. "But when a camel gets angry, it shoots digested food from one of its four stomachs. It pukes at you."

My mom glances at my dad.

"Oh, he's right," he says, nodding. "Though I don't know if I'd call it 'puking.' It's more like 'regurgitating.'"

For once, it's good to have Dad around. Murph could have kept me going on that one for a long time.

In fact, I should probably doubt the part about Chewbacca's voice being a camel's, but instead of giving Murphy the satisfaction of knowing I'm not sure, I change the subject.

"Mom, you're letting Dmitri's dad pass you again," I say.

The Sulls' giant RV roars past us. It's like a gray whale on wheels. A gray whale towing an SUV. Fido stands up in my lap and scratches at the window.

"It's not a race, Rufus," Mom says.

She's wrong, of course. Everything is a race, or can be if you let it. Dmitri and his dad want it to be. They like being the best.

"Dmitri just texted me," Dad says. "It says, 'NYAAH NYAAH!' All in caps."

"Aren't you glad you invited them, Mom?" I ask.

"The more the merrier!" Murph blurts out, totally missing my sarcasm.

Mom smiles at him in the rearview mirror. "Well put, Murphy!"

I may spit like a camel.

"Another text," Dad says, looking at his phone. "It says, 'Rotten egg!!!' Are three exclamation points ever necessary?"

In the mirror, I see Mom's eyes narrow. She flicks on her turn signal.

"We'll see who's a rotten egg!" she says, and guns the motor.

5. We don't rest in the rest area.

We spend our break trying to keep our pets from eating one another.

Most of the terrorizing is done by the puffball. What a demon dog Mars is. Question: What sort of dog has a black tongue? Answer: an evil one.

First thing Mars does is chase Queen Girlisaur up a tree. Good thing Queen Girly is so fast.

"Dogs are supposed to be kept on leashes," Lurena scolds Dmitri, pointing at a sign that says so.

"Whatever, *girl*," Dmitri says.

"She's right," I say. He's so mean that I even end up defending Lurena. "You should leash your puffball, Dmitri, before it kills someone."

Mars stops barking up the tree and turns on Fido, who is angry and nipping at the beast's heels.

"Uh-oh," Dmitri says with a grin.

I'm not worried. Fido can hold her own with Mars. She's done it before. She barks her little head off and snarls with her teeth bared.

Buddy bounds over and gets in between them. Mars adores Buddy, kind of like Dmitri loves Murphy, but Buddy isn't all that interested. She came over to defend Fido. Eventually, the puffball calms down, gives in, then the three of them run off, playing. Dogs are like that.

"You're lucky Mars didn't eat your precious little guinea dog," Dmitri says.

Dmitri is not a dog. He never calms down, or gives in, or plays nice.

He looks at Lurena. "Or your precious little guinea squirrel."

"If Mars ate Queen Girly, I would eat Mars," Lurena says, and licks her lips.

I believe her. She's kind of scary sometimes.

Murphy comes out of his camper with two tennis balls.

"How about a game of Fetch?" he asks.

Dmitri smirks at me. "You're on, Murph!"

He thinks the two balls are for Buddy and Mars, and he's right. But after flipping one of them to Dmitri, Murph digs into his T-shirt pocket and pulls out a neon-green superball. He hasn't forgotten about Fido.

"Here, Buddy!" he calls. "Here, girl!"

Buddy stops what she's doing and gallops toward us, with Mars and Fido in hot pursuit. Murph hurls a tennis ball over Buddy's head, and, without breaking stride, she leaps up and catches it in her mouth. What a dog!

Dmitri throws his ball, and Mars jumps up, but it bonks him on the head.

Murphy tosses the superball to me.

"Here you go, Fido!" I say, and bounce the ball hard off the pavement. It flies up high in the air, so high I can barely see it.

Fido rushes over, then freezes, her head up, watching the ball like a center fielder waiting for a high fly. She gives a little bark as she waits for it to come down. When it does, she jumps up, timing her leap perfectly, and catches the little green ball in her mouth, her plump body twisting in midair. She doesn't land gracefully, probably because she's so plump and her legs are so short, but she's not hurt. She springs to her feet and carries me the ball as if it's a trophy.

"Great catch, girl!" I say.

"She's amazing!" Murphy adds, and slaps me on the back. "Best guinea pig in the whole world!"

"She is something special," Lurena says. "But I'm not sure she's the best." She picks an acorn out of the pocket of her long, frilly skirt. "Watch this." She looks up into the tree where the guinea squirrel is. "Here you go, Queen Girly!" And she underhands the nut up into the air.

Queen Girly fidgets a moment on her branch, as squirrels do, then darts toward the acorn, leaps, snatches it, and lands on a branch below.

"What an acrobat!" Murph says.

"Wow!" I gasp. I'm smiling. I guess I'm proud. Queen Girly's sort of my granddaughter.

"I want her," Dmitri says. "I'll pay you a hundred bucks for her, Lurena."

"No, you won't," she answers.

Dmitri huffs and stomps his foot. It's pretty funny. He's used to getting what he wants, and hates that neither Lurena nor I will give him our guinea pigs. He even went looking for the store where I got Fido—it was called Petopia—but it had closed up and moved away. So he went to a big chain pet store and bought a guinea pig. It didn't act like a dog. Or a squirrel. It acted like a guinea pig. He was very angry—which kind of goes without saying when it comes to Dmitri.

"Mars, come!" Dmitri yells at his dog.

The puffball whimpers. I don't think he wants to come. I wouldn't.

"Mars, *come*!" Dmitri yells again.

Mars backs away.

"You get over here NOW!" Dmitri shouts, and stomps toward his dog.

Mars drops the ball and runs.

Dmitri runs after him, hollering, "Stop! Heel! Mars, you better stop right now! I mean it! Stop!"

"I don't blame Mars," Lurena says. "I wouldn't stop. I'd keep running and running forever to get away from that creep." She shakes her head. "I can't believe your mom invited him, Rufus."

I look at her. I can't believe my mom invited either of them.

"It promises to be a fun trip," I say.

6. White Crappie Lake isn't as bad as it sounds.

It's actually pretty nice. It's surrounded by tree-covered hills. There's a small beach, and a floating pier, and rope swings for diving, and trails for exploring.

The lake is big enough for boats. We don't have a boat, but Murphy's family has a wooden skiff that Murph's dad made. Dmitri's family owns a speedboat, but, since the lake isn't big enough for speedboats, they didn't bring it. They did bring a couple of kayaks, which they hauled on top of the SUV. Dmitri told me they cost more than two thousand dollars each. Not that I asked. I'm looking forward to paddling around in Murph's rowboat. I doubt I'll get to paddle around in Dmitri's kayaks, and I'm fine with that.

The caravan pulls into the campground, Dmitri's RV first. I guess Dmitri's dad wants first pick of the sites available, and that we're rotten eggs. The sites all look alike to me. The four vehicles park side by side, Dmitri's, then Murphy's, then ours, then Lurena's.

Mom hooks us up to the utilities, then asks me to help her open our camper. Fido dives in and out of the camper while we do this.

"She is *so* cute!" my mom squeals.

Mom is different from Dad.

Dad unloads the folding chairs, the charcoal grill, the coolers, then starts setting up his "outdoor kitchen" on a picnic table.

Next door, Murphy and his dad unload their rowboat. His mom sets up the folding chairs and coolers and stuff. Murph's little sister, A.G., is sitting on one of the chairs wrapped in a blanket, no doubt claiming she has some terrible disease no one has ever heard of. That's why she didn't come out of the Jeep at the rest stop. Poor Murph. I'm so glad I don't have a sister.

And I'm so glad Murph is going to be my temporary next-door neighbor!

Lurena's mom and dad are setting up their dome tent while Lurena, their only child, talks to her pets. She's brought along her chinchilla, China C. Hill, her hamster, Sharmet, and, of course, Queen Girlisaur. The names she gives her pets are anagrams of the kinds of animal they are. For example, she mixed up the letters in *chinchilla* and got *China C. Hill*. *Queen Girlisaur* is a rearranged *Guinea Squirrel*. I like anagramming, too. It's one of the two things we have in common. The other is owning rodents. But I'm not into rodents the way Lurena is. I don't actually think of Fido as a rodent.

Lurena has decided to keep her rodents locked in cages at the campground because of what happened at the rest stop (Mars running around free), and because she worries about other animals living in the area: dogs, cats, raccoons, even bears. I hope we see bears. China C. and Sharmet seem worked up, but Queen Girly is going bananas. She's running around her cage and shaking the bars with her tiny fists. My guess is she wants to get out and climb some of the big trees all around us. I wonder if Lurena will let her.

Dmitri's dad pops out of their RV long enough to hook up the utilities. The rest of the family stays inside. That includes Dmitri's older brother, Austin. He didn't come out at the rest stop, probably because, one, he's thirteen and wouldn't want to hang out with a bunch of little kids like us, and, two, he was probably playing video games on the RV's giant flat-screen TV. That's what he's doing now. I can hear muffled gunfire and screams.

The Sulls' RV has not only a TV but also, according to Dmitri (I've never been inside it), a bathroom with a shower, a kitchen with a refrigerator and microwave, plus a washing machine and dryer. I don't think what Dmitri's family is doing is camping. It's more like staying in a mobile hotel room.

As I'm looking at the RV, wondering what they're all doing inside, a long, thin aluminum box attached to the vehicle opens and a blue-and-white-striped awning starts automatically coming out of it. The awning is attached to two struts that hold it up as it unspools.

Right then the side door bursts open and bangs against the side of the RV. Dmitri runs out, wearing only a bathing suit that goes below his knees. It's bright red with a pattern of inky black pictures of angry-looking sharks with their jaws open wide.

"Murph!" he yells, looking right through me, "time for a swim!"

"Shut the door!" his mom's voice yells from inside. "The air-conditioning's on!"

7. "Coatimundi!"

That's what Murphy yells before he lets go of the rope swing and plunges into the lake.

We've been yelling this ever since Murph gave me a tail on a stick for the new bike I got for my birthday. He claimed the tail was from a real coatimundi, an animal that looks like a skinny raccoon and lives in South America, Central America, and southwestern North America. (Never trusting Murphy's stories, I looked it up, and it turns out it's a real animal.) The tail isn't a coatimundi's, or a raccoon's, of course; it's fake. Who sells real animal tails?

Anyway, the word *coatimundi* works real well when you go flying over bike ramps and other kinds of jumps. It's kind of like *Cowabunga!* or *Geronimo!*

When Murph comes out of the water, he hugs himself and shivers.

"Is it cold?" I ask, not seriously. I know it's cold. White Crappie Lake is always cold.

"No," he says, his teeth chattering. "It's like bathwater! Come on in!"

What a con man.

Buddy bounds into the water after him.

"See?" he says. "Buddy's not cold!"

"Buddy has a fur coat," I say.

Fido dives in and dog-paddles after Buddy. I knew Fido could swim. She once fell through a sewer grate and didn't drown (obviously).

"Fido's not cold!" Murph laughs.

"She also has a fur coat."

"I'm not afraid of cold water, Murph!" Dmitri says, and catches hold of the rope.

"I didn't say I was afraid," I say. "I just asked if it was cold."

Mars runs around Dmitri, barking and snapping.

"Back off, Mars!" Dmitri yells at him.

Mars keeps circling.

"Stupid dog," Dmitri mutters, then swings

out over the water. "Cowamundi!" he hollers as he lets go.

No one gave him permission to use our private holler, but I don't mind, since he said it wrong.

He splashes into the water near Murphy.

"It's totally not cold!" he says, trying not to shiver. "Only wimps would think it was cold. Right, Murph?"

Mars runs into the water after him. He swims with his head up. It looks completely ridiculous, this fluffy dog head bobbing above the water.

"Your turn, Roof!" Murph yells.

"Yeah, come on!" Dmitri says. "Don't be a wimp!"

I walk over to the rope.

"Or *do* be a wimp," Lurena's voice says from behind me.

I jump. Not into the water. Just an inch into the air. "Where did you come from?"

"What do you care what Dmitri thinks of you?"

"I actually want to go in the water. I

was going to go in, then he butted in . . ."

"So go in, then."

"Would you like to go first?" I ask, holding out the rope to her.

I know she wouldn't. She's wearing lace-up boots and one of her long, frilly skirts. Is this her idea of camping attire?

"No, thank you," she says. "But I'm not a wimp."

"Neither am I."

"Look at him, Murph," Dmitri yells. "Trying to get a *girl* to go before him! Ha!"

"Do your best to land right on top of him," Lurena says behind her hand.

I smile, then pretend I didn't. I don't want Dmitri seeing me smiling at a girl.

I grip the rope to pull myself off the ground with both hands, back up a few steps, then pull myself up in the air. I stand on the big knot at the end of the rope and start swinging forward, first over the bank, then out over the water. It's fun. Really fun.

"Coatimundi!" I yell, correctly.

For a second, I see them all below me—

Murph, Buddy, Fido, Dmitri, Mars—then, before I've found an opening for me to land, I let go of the rope and belly flop onto Fido.

8. I have no idea how to give CPR to a guinea pig.

Surprisingly, neither does Lurena. But Fido's lying on the bank, not breathing, so I give it a try.

I roll her onto her back, and her mouth falls open. Her eyes are just staring. It's scary. She's soaked to the skin, like she was after she fell in the sewer and Murph and I doused her with a hose. She looks like a drowned rat. What if that's what she *is*?

"Give her CPR! Hurry!" Lurena says. She's soaking wet right down to her lace-up boots. She must have jumped in after I landed on Fido.

Queen Girly is chattering in her cage. Worried about her mom, I guess.

I've seen people giving CPR in movies and on TV shows lots of times. They use two hands and push real hard on a person's chest, which would be excessive when you're dealing with a rodent. I don't want to break her ribs. Or crush her flat. Instead, I set my fingertip where I think her heart is, and press. Nothing happens.

"Puff air into her mouth!" Lurena says.

"Yeah, blow into your rat's mouth." Dmitri laughs.

Lurena slaps him across the arm.

"Hey!" he says.

"Do it, Roof," Murph says. "Breathe into her mouth."

I lean down and place my mouth over Fido's snout. Her fur is bristly, even when wet. She feels cold. Shouldn't she be warm? She's a mammal, after all.

I don't want to explode her lungs, so I puff softly. Nothing happens.

"Harder!" Lurena says.

I puff harder. Nothing.

"More heart massage," she says.

I'm starting to feel real panic. It's like I have

a fever and I'm being stabbed with a thousand little needles in the back, neck, and scalp.

I press down on Fido's chest. She doesn't breathe. I press a bit harder. I puff in her mouth again.

"It's not working!" I shout. "What do I do?"

"Call the pet coroner?" Dmitri says. The creep is actually grinning.

Lurena slaps his arm again and tells him to shut up. I like her in situations like this.

I don't like situations like this.

I scoop Fido off the ground and hold her upside down. I shake her.

"Come on, girl—breathe! *Breathe!*"

She has to start breathing. She has to! If she doesn't, she'll—

"Give her a squeeze," a voice from above us says.

We all look up to see a boy lying on a branch on his stomach, his tan arms and legs dangling. His hair is jet-black.

"Who the heck are you?" Dmitri asks, but I don't care. I'm taking the kid's advice. I'll try anything.

I pick Fido up and squeeze her between my hands, like one of Dad's blue stress balls. Spittle comes out of her mouth, then grows into a bubble.

"Do it again!" Murph says.

I squeeze again, and the bubble pops. I feel Fido wiggle slightly and take a shuddery breath. She's alive!

"She moved!" I say.

"Hurray!" Murph cheers. Lurena claps rapidly.

I'm so relieved I might cry. I blink fast to wipe any tears away. Dmitri sees them anyway.

"Aw, Wufus is cwying ovew his widdew wat!"

"Do I need to slap you again?" Lurena asks.

His smirk turns to a sneer. "You better not!"

I cup Fido in my hands as if she's an egg.

"You all right?" I whisper.

She coughs a few times, then wriggles to her feet. Her tongue spills out. She pants.

"I'm so sorry. I didn't see you."

"I never saw a guinea pig swim," the boy in the tree says.

"That's not all she does," Lurena says, and winks at me.

"You saved her life," Murph says, then asks, "What's your name?"

"Pablo."

"Pablo?" Dmitri says with a snicker.

"Yes," Pablo says. "What's your name?"

"None of your business, *Pablo*."

It's so like Dmitri to be rude at hello. How can he tell from here that Pablo is someone he won't like? Is it just his name? Names aren't our faults. They're our parents'. Besides, what's wrong with the name *Pablo*?

"I'm Murphy," Murph says. "And this is Rufus, and the one you saved is Fido."

"Hi," I say. "Thanks so much. I thought she was a goner."

Fido looks up at the boy and barks.

"I'm Lurena," Lurena says. "So you're camping here?"

"Uh-huh," the boy says. "We've been here a couple days. Me and my family."

"Does your family hang around in trees and spy on people, too?" Dmitri asks.

Is that it? He doesn't like Pablo because he's in a tree and spying? What's wrong with either of those things? I like doing both.

"That's Dmitri," Lurena says, scowling at him. "He follows us around, bugging us and being a jerk. Just ignore him."

"Is that your black chow chow?" Pablo asks him.

"He's not a 'chow chow,'" Dmitri says. "He's a chow, and you better be careful or he'll rip you up."

"Good thing I'm in a tree," Pablo says.

Murphy laughs. "He's right, you know, Dmitri. Technically, Mars is a chow chow."

Dmitri fumes but doesn't object. He's too interested in becoming Murph's best friend to object.

"Come on down, Pablo," Murph says. "Swim with us."

"Yeah," I say over Dmitri's groans. "The more the merrier."

9. Pablo doesn't swim.

He doesn't come out and say it, but it's obvious. Maybe he doesn't know how. Maybe he thinks the water is too cold. Maybe he's scared. But he doesn't get in the water.

"You don't want to jump from the rope swing, Pablo?" Murph asks.

He and I and Dmitri are back in the water with the dogs, including Fido. I'm proud of her for diving right back in after our collision.

"Or maybe swim out to the floating pier?" I suggest. "There's a diving board on it."

"No, thanks," Pablo says with his hands in the back pockets of his shorts. He came down from the tree and is standing on the shore with Lurena. He doesn't seem afraid. He seems relaxed.

"I bet he can't swim," Dmitri says, then laughs. "Can you believe that? A kid his age that can't swim?"

"Remember what I said about him," Lurena says to Pablo. "Would you like to see my pets? I have a guinea pig, too. She's Fido's daughter, in fact, and she acts just like a squirrel. Her name is Queen Girlisaur."

"The guinea squirrel should be mine!" Dmitri yells.

Which is his opinion, no one else's.

"Come on, Pablo," Lurena says. "I'll show you all my rodents. You can meet China C. Hill, my chinchilla. And Sharmet, my hamster . . ."

Her voice fades as she and Pablo walk away toward her family's tent.

"That kid's a dorkchop," Dmitri says. "Right, Murph?"

"Seems nice to me," Murph says. "Come on. Let's swim out to the pier."

He starts swimming, and Dmitri and I splash after him.

"Last one there's a rotten egg!" Dmitri yells.

Again with the rotten egg.

"How could an egg swim?" I ask.

"They can't. That's why they lose!"

"What are you if you're the first one there? A fresh egg?"

"Shut up and swim."

I can't decide if I want to try to beat him to the pier or drop back and take my time. I don't like competing with him. I don't like *being* with him.

I glance back and see the dogs swimming after us. Fido's moving pretty fast for such a little thing.

I decide to wait for them. Dogs don't call anyone rotten eggs.

When Fido catches up to me, she climbs up onto my back. I keep paddling as she settles on the base of my neck for a rest. I do the breaststroke so I won't knock her off.

"Rotten egg!" Dmitri says from the pier, when I finally arrive.

"I think he's a good egg," Murph says with a British accent. "A right good egg, 'e is."

Good old Murph.

I climb up the ladder with Fido on my

shoulder. Murphy and Dmitri lug their heavy, scrambling, soaking wet hounds up onto the pier. Mars looks ridiculous, with his puffy head sitting on top of his drenched body.

We start running off the diving board, doing cannonballs and flips. Murph pretends to walk off the end accidentally, yelping and flailing his arms and legs all the way to the water. I dive in to "save" him.

"I can't—blub!—I can't swim—blub, blub!" he shouts, saying the word *blub* as if he's reading it from a book.

"Like Pablo, right, Murph?" Dmitri says, then bounces high off the board and, instead of diving into the water, belly flops with a loud *THAP!*

When he comes back up, his face is red.

"Didn't hurt at all," he says, grimacing.

"Glad to hear it," I say.

Then the dogs dive in.

I'm having a good time.

10. Dad doesn't like *hot* dogs, either.

He says he doesn't trust them. There's no telling where the meat comes from, he says. They're filled with nasty chemicals and dyes. They're slimy.

Here are some other normal cookout foods Dad doesn't trust:

- Cheeseburgers (mad cow disease)
- Potato chips (deep-fried foods are fatty and contain too much sodium)
- Potato salad (mayonnaise goes bad in the sun)
- Pork and beans (more weird meat)
- Soda (way too much sugar)
- Marshmallows (all sugar)

- S'mores (marshmallows and chocolate, so double sugar)

For dinner, he sets out weighty, whole-wheat buns, slices of tasteless soy cheese, and brown—not yellow—mustard. When I walk up, he opens the grill, scrapes a big mushroom off the grate, and offers the sweaty, blackened thing to me.

Fido jumps up onto the picnic table, sniffing the air. When she smells the mushroom, she turns up her nose.

I've been swimming all afternoon. I'm tired, sunburned, and, most of all, starving. I don't want a fungus.

"Seriously?" I say to Dad. "A mushroom? At a cookout?"

"You want something else?" he asks.

"What else you got?"

"Grilled eggplant and grilled yam wedges. They're better than French fries, believe me."

I don't believe him, and I can't believe this is his idea of a cookout. Eggplant? Come on!

"Hey, Roof!" Murphy calls from over by

the campfire. We have one big community fire for all four families. "Let's roast us some dogs!"

He holds up a package of hot dogs and two sharpened sticks. He knows what my dad considers food. He's bailing me out.

Fido dives off the table and zooms over to him. It may be the fastest I've ever seen her run. I follow after her.

"No offense, Art!" Murph calls to my dad. "I'm sure your dinner is delicious!"

Dad waves his spatula. "None taken."

Nobody can ever be sore at Murphy Molloy.

"Thank you, thank you, thank you!" I say as I take a stick. "The guy made grilled mushrooms and eggplant, if you can believe it."

"Eggplant? Wow. Your dad's one in a million."

"Yeah. I won the lottery when I got him."

Murph elbows me and laughs. "Here, take a dog."

I do. It's pretty slimy, before you roast it, that is. I poke it with my stick, then Murph and I sit with our dogs in the fire. What's better than roasting hot dogs over a campfire? Not much.

Fido scampers around my feet, whining.

"No begging," I say. "I'll give you one in your bowl."

"Aw, here," Murph says, holding out the hot dog package. "Give her one. It's a campout."

He's right. We're cooking outside with dirty sticks over an open flame. We're going to eat dinner outside. This is no time for house rules.

I take out a dog and hand it to Fido. She snatches it in her paws and starts gnawing on it. Guinea pigs don't usually eat meat, but Fido's not your usual guinea pig.

Lurena walks up with a plate. "Mind if I sit down?" she asks.

Yes.

"Not at all," Murph says. "What have you got there?"

"A portobello sandwich and some grilled veggies, courtesy of Art. The man's a wizard with a grill." She nibbles a yam wedge. "Mm, just scrumptious!"

"They do look good," Murph says. "Can I try one?"

Is he serious?

"Absolutely," Lurena says. "They're much better than French fries."

Is she serious?

"Would you like one, Rufus?" she asks.

"You should, Roof," Murph says, chewing one. "They're tasty."

Tasty is not a word he would use if he liked the yam wedge.

"Thanks, no," I say. "Saving room for about a hundred hot dogs."

Dmitri walks up. What's better than a wienie roast with Lurena and Dmitri? A wienie roast without them.

"What's up, Murph?" he asks, then squeezes between us on the log. He's holding a stick with a giant hot dog pierced on it. I've heard of a foot-long dog before, but this one's a foot and a half, and three inches thick. It's like a rolling pin made of meat. I'm jealous.

"Rufus just said he could eat a hundred hot dogs," Murph says.

"Yeah?" Dmitri says. "I could eat two hundred."

"If you do, I'll give you Queen Girly," Lurena says.

"You're on!" Dmitri says.

Murph says, "You know, I read online just yesterday that the world record for eating hot dogs, with buns, is sixty-eight. This kid named Chestnut won."

"His name was *Chestnut*?" I ask.

"It was his last name. Something Chestnut." Yeah, right.

"I could do that easy," Dmitri says. "Except that the hot dogs my mom buys are so ginormous."

"I'll trade with you," I say.

"Excellent solution!" Murph says. "Trade with Roof. And don't worry, we have plenty more normal-size hot dogs. I think my mom brought a dozen packages. That's like, what? Two hundred dogs?"

Murph's not so hot at math. I had to tutor him so he didn't fail it this year. He didn't fail it.

"Eight in a package," I say, "times twelve. That's ninety-six dogs, Murph."

"Well, that's still plenty."

"Why don't I trade with *you*, Murph?" Dmitri asks.

Obviously, he doesn't want to give his monster dog to me.

"Because I'll be competing right alongside you!" Murph says.

"And I won't be," I say.

Dmitri shakes his head slightly. "Figures. Chicken."

"No, not chicken. I just don't feel like stuffing myself with hot dogs till I puke."

I swap sticks with him. Considering the size of the thing now at the end of my stick, I will be stuffing myself with hot dogs after all.

"Thanks," I say. "Good luck breaking the record."

"I won't need luck," he grunts. "I have skill."

"Well, good skill, then."

11. Dmitri can't keep the sixth one down.

Then the other five start coming back up. He runs off to the woods to take care of that.

The giant hot dog he gave me, by the way, was delicious.

"So he doesn't get Queen Girly after all," Lurena says, smiling.

"He came so close," Murph says.

"He ate five," I say. "The record's sixty-eight. That's close?"

"You didn't let me finish. What I was going to say was 'He came so close to puking all over us.'"

"Thank goodness he didn't," Lurena says.

"What happened to Dummy?" a voice says behind us.

We turn around. Dmitri's brother, Austin, is walking toward us.

"Who's Dummy?" Lurena asks. "Do you mean Dmitri?"

"Yeah, I've always called him Dummy. Like, short for Dmitri?"

Austin is taller and skinnier than Dmitri, but they're definitely brothers. Austin has the same sharp nose and chin, and mean mouth.

"Funny," Lurena says sarcastically.

"Thanks," Austin says. "So why'd Dummy go running off to the woods? He got the runs? Get it? Running because he has the runs?"

"Also funny," Lurena says with an eye roll.

"Are you Dummy's girlfriend?" Austin asks.

"Now, that's *not* funny," Lurena says, and stands up. "Excuse me." She walks away.

"Wow," Austin says. "She's cool. Cool as a campfire. Right?" He snorts.

"Good one," I say. I don't know why. It wasn't. In fact, I'm not even sure I get it.

"Let's go find Pablo," Murph says, saving me.

"Yes, let's," I say.

"Who's Pablo?" Austin asks.

"A new friend of ours," Murph says.

"Well, give me the hot dogs before you go, dude," Austin says, pointing at the package on the log between Murph and me.

"There's only one left, but it's all yours, Awesome Austin," Murph says, and hands the package to him.

Austin laughs. "That's good, man. 'Awesome Austin.' I never thought of that. Nice work, dude." He slaps Murph on the shoulder.

Everyone likes Murph. Sometimes I wonder if that's a good thing.

We go looking for Pablo's camp. The night is warm and clear. Stars peek through the treetops, and fireflies float around us like little stars. The campground smells of smoke, meat, and citronella. People are gathered around fires, talking and laughing, or are inside tents with lanterns, their silhouettes fluttering. Kids are running around with flashlights, whispering and giggling, looking for animals or ghosts. Dad doesn't know what he's talking about: camping is great.

We don't see Pablo anywhere, so Murph calls out his name, cupping his hands around his mouth. Does that really make your voice carry farther? I try it with cupped hands, then without, and realize there's no way for me to tell.

"I'm over here," Pablo answers.

We find him reading with a flashlight on a lounge chair outside a gigantic white RV. It's bigger than Dmitri's. Sections of it slide out like big dresser drawers, which make it even bigger. The lights are all on inside.

"This your rig, Pablo?" Murph asks.

Pablo looks confused, then realizes what Murph means. "Yeah, it's ours."

"Does it have a spa?" Murph asks.

"A spa?"

"Kidding," Murph says with a laugh. "Want to come over to our campfire and roast s'mores with us?"

I'm sure glad Mom invited Murphy's family. Otherwise, we wouldn't have marshmallows, not to mention s'mores.

Pablo looks down at his book, like he's torn

between s'mores and reading. Is that really a choice?

"Uh . . . sure," he says. "Let me tell my parents I'm going."

He opens the door and steps up into the RV. We hear him inside saying something in another language (I think Spanish), then we hear a woman (probably his mom) answer in the same language. Then he comes back out.

"Okay. Let's go."

"What were you reading?" I ask as we walk.

"*Twenty Thousand Leagues Under the Sea*," Pablo says.

"Is it good?" Murph asks.

"Really good."

"What's it about?" I ask.

"In the beginning, everybody thinks some monster is attacking all these ships at sea, but they're wrong. You want me to spoil it for you?"

"No," we both say.

"The writing is sort of old-fashioned. Like *Treasure Island*. Did you ever read that one? It's about pirates."

"I've read it," Murph says. "You know, for a

kid who doesn't like water, you read a lot of books about the sea."

Pablo shrugs.

"I brought a rowboat," Murph says. "Do you want to go out in it with us tomorrow? It seats three."

"No, thanks," Pablo says. He kicks a rock. "I like reading about boats and stuff, but I'm not so into being . . . *in* them."

"Do you know how to swim?" I ask.

It gets quiet a moment, then Murph says, "Let's get some s'mores before my sister devours them all. The girl's a marshmallow *fiend*."

Pablo looks back over his shoulder. "So is my sister. Plus, she taps on my aquariums all the time. Which drives me crazy."

Another quiet moment.

"Aquariums?" I finally ask. "Plural?"

Before Pablo can answer, Murph yells, "S'mores!" and takes off running.

We follow him.

12. Solar energy from the moon.

That's what Murphy claims scientists are currently working on.

"They want to put up solar panels all over the moon's surface," he says. "Just cover the whole moon with them."

We're sitting on the beach—Murph, Pablo, Buddy, Fido, and me—looking up at the moon, which is a little less than full. Even so, it's lighting up the lake like a giant flashlight.

"How will they get the energy to Earth?" Pablo asks.

"That's the tricky part," Murph says. "They're thinking very long extension cords."

Pablo and I groan.

"What?" Murph says.

"It's a long way to the moon," I say. "Really long."

"Two hundred thirty-eight thousand nine hundred miles," Pablo says.

Murph and I look at him.

"That's the average distance, of course," Pablo says. "It changes during the course of the moon's orbit. It's closer at the perigee and farther at the apogee."

"How do you know all this?" I ask him.

"I don't know," he says. "I just do."

"It wouldn't work even if the scientists did have extension cords that long, because both the Earth and the moon are spinning," I say. "The cords would get all tangled up."

"I'm just telling you what I heard," Murph says. "Read, actually. In *National Geographic*."

I roll my eyes. "Don't believe him, Pablo. He's always making stuff up. It's his idea of fun."

"I only speak the truth," Murph says as he picks up a stick and hurls it down the beach. Buddy and Fido tear after it.

"I've never seen a guinea pig play Fetch," Pablo says. "Did you train her yourself?"

"No. She came that way. From the pet store."

"Did she cost extra?"

"My mom bought her, and I don't think she had any idea Fido acted like a dog."

"Which store? I wouldn't mind having one myself."

Murph laughs. "You and everyone else at our school!"

"So the store doesn't have any more?" Pablo asks.

"It's kind of a long story," I say. "You see, my dad wouldn't let me have a dog. . . . It's hard to believe, but he doesn't like dogs . . . so my mom bought me a guinea pig. My dad didn't like the guinea pig, either. . . . He doesn't like a lot of things . . . so he said we had to bring it back to the store. But the store wasn't there anymore. It had closed up and moved away."

"That's weird," Pablo says.

"Tell me about it. So then I discover Fido acts like a dog, and pretty soon word gets out, and everyone at school wants one . . ."

"Including me," Murph says.

"But especially Dmitri," I say. "Boy, does he want one!"

Right then Buddy starts growling.

"What is it, girl?" Murph calls out. "What do you see?"

"Isn't she just growling at Fido?" Pablo asks.

"It's a different growl," I say. I like that I can tell Buddy's growls apart. "It's an intruder growl. Must be another animal."

"Probably just a strange dog," Murph says.

We go over to check and hear a peeping sound, like a bird, then a splash. A sleek, dark animal swims away from the bank, its head above the water. Buddy barks, and it dives under the surface. A long, thick tail is the last thing we see.

"An otter," Murph says.

There are always otters at the lake.

Fido growls. She has the stick in her mouth. She beat out Buddy for it!

"Good girl!" I say, petting her head. I pry the stick out of her mouth and throw it. She and Buddy run after it.

"So Fido had a baby that acts like a squirrel?" Pablo asks.

"Yeah. She must have been pregnant when Mom bought her. It was weird, because I wanted a dog and got a guinea pig that acted like one, and Lurena wanted a squirrel and she got a guinea pig that acted like one."

"I like tropical fish," Pablo says. "I wonder what I'd get."

"No point in wondering, unless you can find a Petopia," Murph says.

"What's a Petopia?"

"Petopia is the name of the store where my mom bought Fido," I say. "But it disappeared."

"I think I saw one on the way here," Pablo says.

Murph and I gasp at the same time, then both say, "Where?"

"Jinx!" Murph says, then starts counting.

"Idaho Jinx," I say, and he stops. That's how we work jinxes.

"I'm not exactly sure," Pablo says. "It was in a mini-mall, I think. I saw a sign—"

"Was it far from here?" I ask. "Which way did you come from?"

"We live in Mechanicsburg. West of here."

"We came from Rustbury, which is the other way." I look at Murph.

"So we wouldn't have passed it," he says.

"Right. Are you sure it said Petopia? Not something else? There are lots of pet stores with really punny names ..."

"Like Pawsitively Pets," Murphy says. "That's a pet store in Wheeling ..."

"I'm sure," Pablo says. "In fact, I'm *paws*itive."

Murph laughs.

"I'll ask my parents to stop there on our way home," Pablo says. "I'll tell them I want to see what fish they carry."

"But the store will be gone by then!" Murph shouts. "We have to go sooner."

Whoa. I hadn't realized how much he wants a guinea dog. I don't know why he does. He has the best *actual* dog in the whole world.

"Maybe we could go tomorrow," I say. "We'd just have to talk someone's parents into taking us."

"I don't know if my mom or dad would want to go looking for a pet store," Murph says. "Maybe if I told them Pablo saw a Petopia . . ."

"Well, *my* dad won't do it," I say.

"How about your mom?" Murph says. "Wouldn't she be excited to find another Petopia?"

She might be at that. She's pretty pleased with herself for bringing home such a special guinea pig. I'm pretty pleased with her, too.

"I'll ask, but we'd have to sneak away without Dad seeing us."

"If you found the store, what sort of pet would you look for?" Pablo asks. "Another guinea pig?"

"I'd sure like one," Murph says.

"So would Lurena," I say.

"And Dmitri," Murph and I say together.

"Jinx," Murph says. "One, two, three . . ."

"Idaho Jinx," I say. "Listen, Pablo, we can't let Dmitri know you saw a Petopia, okay?"

"Why?" Pablo asks.

Why don't I want Dmitri to get his own guinea dog? Good question. Is it because his parents give him everything he wants? Because he's spoiled rotten and a big show-off? Because he bought a guinea pig and when it didn't act like a dog, he didn't want it anymore? Because he's mean and—

"Hey, Murph!" Dmitri calls from behind us. "What are you doing? I've been looking for you everywhere! Didn't you hear me calling? Why are you hanging out with these two losers?"

"That's why," I say to Pablo.

13. Adults, rodent cages, and a girl in a long skirt.

That's what Murph, Dmitri, and I find around the campfire when we return. None of them is my idea of fun.

What I want to do is have a word with my mom. I want to tell her about Petopia, but I don't want my dad, Lurena, or Dmitri to hear. Unfortunately, all the parents, plus Lurena, are sitting around the campfire. My mom loves parties, which is probably one of the reasons that she invited the other two families. I'm sure to her a campout is just an excuse for a big barbecue. I know she wanted to get to know Lurena's and Dmitri's parents better. Murph's she's known for years. Why wasn't she content with that?

When we walk up, she's in the middle of telling a story.

"So I put the can in the paint shaker ..." Mom works in the paint department at a hardware store. ". . . Did I mention it was pink? That this man wanted pink paint? Did I say that?"

"You did, Raquel," Dad says without emotion. "You mentioned it thrice."

Dmitri's dad, Scott, is leaning back in his chair, smiling, one leg crossed horizontally over the other. He's shaking his foot like it's a dog's happy tail. I don't know what keeps his flip-flop from flying off. His wife, Carol, is not smiling. Her face is wearing a frown and an awful lot of makeup for a camping trip. She pretends to be listening to Mom's story, but mostly she keeps stealing looks at her phone. She's not wearing a watch. I think she's checking the time.

"Okay, *Art*," Mom goes on. "For the *fourth* time, it was pink ... *so* pink ... like a sunburned flamingo."

Scott laughs.

Carol doesn't.

"I can't imagine what they were planning to paint with it! Maybe a . . . a . . ."

"A baby's room?" Billie asks. Billie is Murph's mom. She's sitting next to my mom.

Murph's dad, Sam, is poking at the fire with a stick. I get the feeling he's the one who keeps it burning. He's good at useful things like that.

Lurena's parents are there, too. Her dad, Jimmy, has this habit of running his fingers through his very curly brown hair, which causes it to stand on end and make him look like a clown. Someone should tell him. His wife, Elaine, has straight blond hair that goes down to her waist, like Lurena's, only whiter. She doesn't wear old-timey clothes, though. She's wearing normal clothes, including a white T-shirt with words on it. Her hair hides most of the letters, so I can't read what it says.

Both of them are pretty normal, unlike their daughter. I wonder where she gets the weirdness from. Then again, my parents are both weird, and I turned out normal. Where did

I get my normalness from? Maybe weirdness and normalness aren't passed down, like eye color is.

Lurena is sitting on the ground between her parents' chairs, peering in through the bars at her pets and talking to them in a high voice. I can't make out what she's saying over my mom's loud story, which is a relief.

"But this isn't baby-room, pastel pink," Mom says. "This is *hot* pink. Anyway, I put the paint can in the shaker and I . . ." She laughs into her palm. "I was *positive* I'd hammered the lid on good and tight. I mean, I shake hundreds of cans of paint a day. I *never* forget."

"No!" Scott says.

"I can see where this is going!" Billie says.

"So—*splat!*" Mom says, spreading her fingers really fast.

Everyone but Dad and Carol laughs. Dad's heard it before. Carol is doing something on her phone.

"Luckily, the Plexiglas door was shut, but it was instantly painted hot pink, and then paint oozed out from around the edges. It looked like Pepto-Bismol. It took a full hour to clean it all up."

Jimmy asks, "So you mixed them up another can of pink paint?"

Mom says yes by lifting her eyebrows. "We have two shakers."

Everybody nods.

Her story is over. I'm hoping someone else will tell the next one, so I can steal her away.

"That's a sweet canoe you got there, Sammy," Jimmy says to Murph's dad, whose name is Sam, not Sammy.

"It's a skiff," Sam says. "But thanks."

Dmitri's mom sighs aloud, then stands up. "I'm ready to turn in. Good night, all." She walks away.

"Can I have more s'mores, Mom?" Dmitri calls after her.

"Whatever," she says, without turning around.

Dmitri starts putting one together.

"How about me, Mom?" Murph asks Billie. "Can I have s'more s'mores?" He beams at her.

"How many have you had?" she asks.

"One?"

More like six.

"Okay, but only one more," his mom says.

Everyone lets Murph slide. Especially his mom.

I look at my mom. She looks at my dad. I look at my dad. I don't have to ask. It's n'more s'mores for me.

"I need to marinate some vegetables for breakfast," Dad says, and leaves the circle.

Here's my chance.

I jump into his seat and whisper in Mom's ear, "I need to tell you something."

"Okay," she says. "What is it?"

I look around the circle. Nothing like whispering to get everyone's attention.

Murph holds up a stick he has stuck about eight marshmallows on.

"One more s'more!" he says with a laugh.

This distracts everyone long enough for me to tell my mom what Pablo saw.

14. The only way to get one off you is to chop off its head.

That's how the story always goes. The beast sleeps at the bottom of the lake or pond, waiting, then you come by and—*chomp!*—it bites down on your ankle and refuses to let go, no matter what you do. You can drag it out of the water and beat it with a stick, and it won't let go. You can't pry its jaws open with a crowbar. The only thing you can do is cut off its head.

It's an old story, one I've heard all my life: the story of the giant alligator snapping turtle in the lake (or pond). And I'm hearing it again, this time from Dmitri.

"You're smart to stay out of the water,"

Dmitri says to Pablo. "You don't want one of those things to get you."

We've all come down to the beach to launch the boats. Dmitri's dad and brother are in the two kayaks, paddling away. Murph and his dad are carrying the skiff into the water. Buddy's swimming around them. Fido's chasing Buddy. Dmitri, Pablo, Lurena, and I are sitting together on the bank.

"It happened to a friend of mine back in Irondale," Dmitri says.

Dmitri moved to Rustbury this year, from Irondale, which, according to him, was better than Rustbury in every way possible. I guess having confirmed alligator-snapping-turtle attacks is another example.

"I think turtle attacks are just urban myths," Pablo says. "Did you actually see the turtle's head after they chopped it off?"

"No," Dmitri says, rolling his eyes. "The doctors didn't *keep* it. They destroyed it. That's what they do. Don't you know any-thing?"

"I know some things," Pablo says. "I

know when someone is making stuff up, and when he's being insulting."

Lurena and I laugh.

Dmitri's face turns red.

A bunch of ducks squawks suddenly and starts flapping out onto the lake. It's Fido. She can't leave ducks alone.

"Fido, come!" I say.

"You really should keep her on a leash," Lurena says. "They have signs up about it."

"They say to keep your *dog* on a leash," I say. "Fido's not a dog."

"She's frightening the wildlife."

Fido pads up to me, her tongue hanging out.

"Should I keep her in a cage?" I ask as I bend down to pet her.

The ducks settle down and float peacefully on the water. Then Mars woofs and plunges in. The ducks squawk again and flap and splash.

"That one should definitely be on a leash," Lurena says.

"He's on vacation, too," Dmitri says. "I'm not going to put him on a leash." He stands up. "Hey, Murph! You ready for me?"

I don't know why he thinks Murph is going to let him go instead of me. Murph and I are best friends, and have been since kindergarten. Dmitri can wait for one of the kayaks.

But then I think about Pablo, staying here on the shore with Lurena and the cages. Plus, I want to tell him what my mom said.

"Roof's going first!" Murph calls back.

Good old Murph.

"It's okay," I say. "I'll wait."

Dmitri smacks my arm with the back of his hand. "Thanks," he says, then adds, "sucker!"

He runs into the water toward the skiff, Mars on his heels.

"You didn't have to stay with me," Pablo says.

"I know." I glance at Lurena. I don't want her to know about Petopia. "So what do you like to do here, since you don't go into the water?"

"I look for shells and stuff," he says, "to put in my aquariums."

"How many aquariums do you have?" Lurena asks.

"Three," he says.

"Big ones?" I ask.

"Two are just twenty-gallon tanks. One is a thirty-gallon hexagonal."

"Do you have any sharks?"

"A couple."

"Cool. Let's go look for some shells and stuff," I say, hoping Lurena won't want to join us.

"I know a good spot," she says.

Of course she does.

15. Lurena the Pest.

That's what I'd call a book about her.

She shows up places uninvited. She invites herself. And she won't leave, no matter what I say. Here are some examples of what I've said in the past:

- "I was just heading out."
- "Murphy's coming over."
- "I have a ton of homework to do."
- "My dad says I have to mow the lawn."
- "I have a terrible headache."
- "I have laryngitis." (I wrote this down.)
- "I have mad cow disease."
- "Fido is a carrier of rodent flu."
- "A guy's coming over with his pet grizzly bear that eats girls."

- "Our house is being demolished today, so . . ."
- "I think I'm allergic to you."
- "I'm going to throw up."
- "I think you need to leave now."
- "Leave, Lurena. Now!"
- "Just *go* already!"
- "I'm calling the police if you don't leave."
- "Get lost!"
- "OUT!"

She doesn't take hints very well.

She leads Pablo and me to the spot she talked about. It's a small, rocky beach. We start poking around for shells.

"What do you like about fish?" Lurena asks Pablo.

"I don't know," he says.

"Do you like that they're so sparkly and colorful and pretty?"

Like that's what a boy would like about anything.

"Sure," he says.

He's just being agreeable.

"Do you like their big eyes and their big kissy mouths?"

That's too much!

"Seriously?" I say. " 'Kissy mouths'? Pablo is a boy, Lurena."

"What does that mean? Boys can't appreciate a kissy mouth?"

"I just like watching them," Pablo says. "They make me feel calm."

"Yes," Lurena says. "They are calming. And serene. And tranquilizing. *So* tranquilizing."

"What are you, a thesaurus?" I ask.

"Why do you like rodents?" Pablo asks her.

"Oh, for so many reasons, Pablo. Thanks for asking. They're soft and furry, of course. And adorable. And cute. And cuddly. And—"

"Thesaurus," I say under my breath.

"And they're loyal. *So* loyal. My rodents *love* me."

I guess someone has to.

"And they talk to me. They tell me they love me."

"They *tell* you?" I ask.

"Of course they do!"

"What are they saying now?" Pablo asks.

She leans over her hamster's cage.

"They say they love me oodles and oodles."

"I'm going to throw up," I say.

"Doesn't Fido talk to you?" Lurena asks.

"Nope. My guinea pig doesn't speak to me. Isn't that strange?"

"Maybe she doesn't love you." She winks.

I stay calm. Serene. Tranquil.

"I think I hear your mom calling you," I say.

"I think I hear Queen Girly calling her mom," Pablo says.

True, the guinea squirrel is whining in her cage, and Fido is running around it, also whining.

"Can't you let her out for a while?" Pablo asks Lurena.

"She might run up a tree. There might be raccoons in the tree," Lurena says, still poking through the rocks. "Here's a good one, Pablo." She holds out a shell to him.

Fido grips the bars of Queen Girly's cage and shakes them.

"Maybe you could let Fido *in*," Pablo suggests.

Lurena thinks about this, then says, "Okay. But help me. I don't want Queen Girly escaping."

We huddle around the cage in case the guinea squirrel tries to make a break for it, while Lurena unlatches the cage door and opens it a crack. Queen Girly does try to get out, just as Fido scrambles to get in. With some effort, Lurena is able to push Fido in, then relock the door.

"What's Queen Girly saying now?" Pablo asks.

Lurena cups her ear. "She says, 'Thanks, Lurena. I love you so much!'"

Oh, brother.

16. 2 guys + 2 dogs + 1 skiff = fun x 5 trillion.

Especially when the guys are Murphy and me and the dogs are Buddy and Fido.

Lurena stays with Pablo.

"I couldn't get rid of her," I say to Murph as I row. "She just sticks to me like glue. Like barnacles, more like. Lurena's a barnacle."

Murph laughs. "I'll get her to come out in the skiff with me. She can even bring her cages. The more the—"

"It isn't merrier to me to have Lurena around. It isn't even merry. But I'm sure you'll have a merry voyage with her and her rodents."

He laughs again. I don't know what he finds funny, but his laughing makes me laugh, too. He has that effect on people. It's hard to stay grouchy around him, even when you want to.

He lies back, his arms bent at the elbows, his hands in the water.

"Ahhhhh!" he says. "This is the life, ain't it, Tom?"

"It ain't bad, Huck," I answer. I read the book *Tom Sawyer* this year after Murph recommended it. He's like Pablo: he likes old books. The characters in the book spoke funny, but I got used to it.

"We should just drift away forever," he says. "Drift all the way downriver to Jamaica and lay in the sun all day, eating coconuts."

"Sounds like heaven, Huck," I say. "But this here's a lake, not a river."

"Well, it ain't bad here, neither."

"No, it ain't."

"Paddle us 'round the lake a couple times, will you, Tom? That'd be ever so kind of you."

"It'd be my pleasure, Huckleberry."

"Let me know if you spot any alligators or snappy turtles, and I'll help you wrassle 'em."

"Will do. Say, Huck, ain't those ducks over there poisonous?"

Murph once tried to persuade me that a flock of poisonous ducks had landed in our town. I didn't believe him, but I did go to our local lake with him, just to check. There were ducks on it, but they weren't poisonous.

Murph sits up, shades his eyes. "Where, Tom?"

I point to a flock of ducks floating off, starboard side.

Fido, who'd been curled up in the hull with Buddy, napping, perks up. She rushes up onto my lap, sets her paws on the gunwale, barks, then dives into the lake and starts swimming in the direction of the ducks. The ducks quack and scatter.

"That's a fine bird dog you got there, Tom."

"Thanks, Huck."

Buddy, seeing Fido jump overboard, gets to her feet and growls.

"Easy there, girl," Huck ... I mean Murphy ... says. "Don't rock the boat now ..."

But Buddy does rock the boat. She rises up on her hind legs, sets her forepaws on the gunwale, and woofs a big *woof*. What a dog!

Then her hind legs start scrambling around the hull, trying to find a foothold, and the boat starts rocking. Before Murph can tell her to sit, her paws slip off the gunwale, she falls hard onto her chest, the boat tips, Murph and I fall over sideways, and we capsize. The boat lands upside down over us. Buddy sniffs and paws at the outside, whimpering. We reach up and grab hold of the bench seats.

"Thought I might go for a swim, Tom," Murph says, grinning.

"Thought I'd join you, Huck," I say.

Fido pops up out of the water between us, soaked to the skin. She looks at Murph, then twists around and looks at me.

"Your bird dog is here to rescue us, Tom," Murph says.

"Yup, she sure is, Huck."

17. Tom Sawyer dries off in the gigantic RV.

He changes into some of Pablo's clothes in the master bedroom, then Pablo's mom puts Tom's clothes in the dryer.

"This place is amazing," I say.

Pablo's RV is like Dmitri's: it has the washer and dryer, a bathroom, a fridge, a microwave, and a big flat-screen TV. It's like a mobile hotel room. I guess Pablo's family has a lot of money, too. But Pablo acts a lot differently from Dmitri. A *lot* differently.

We're sitting at the kitchen table, which is in the part of the RV that slides out. His mom puts a bowl of tortilla chips and a plastic container of salsa on the table. Fido sits on the floor, begging.

"Quiet!" I say to her.

She stops whining.

"Thank you, Mrs. . . ."

"Covarrubias," she says.

It's pretty, but I can't say it. I smile instead.

"You can call her Yolanda," Pablo says.

"*Sí,*" she says, with a big smile. "Yolanda."

Pablo pronounced it, *Yo-lan-da*, but she said, *Jo-lan-da*.

"Thank you, Yolanda," I say, with a *y* sound, since I don't speak Spanish.

She nods, then speaks to Pablo in Spanish. He nods and answers in Spanish. Then she goes outside.

"It's cool you speak Spanish," I say.

"Thanks," he says. "My parents were born in Mexico. I was born in Mechanicsburg. My sister, too. My parents don't speak very much English. Most of their friends and co-workers speak Spanish. My sister and I speak it to them, too. So they don't learn English."

"So it's cool you speak English, too," I say. I feel like the things I'm saying are sort of stupid. None of my friends speaks another language, so this is new to me.

"Yeah," Pablo says.

We quietly eat a few chips. That is, we don't talk; you can't eat tortilla chips quietly. The salsa turns out to be very hot. Pablo gobbles it up anyway. My lips are on fire.

Fido whines again.

"Can I give her one?" I ask Pablo.

He says, "Sure," so I drop a chip—without salsa—on the floor. Fido crunches it.

"We'd better get going," I say, "while Murph and Lurena are still in the skiff."

After we got the boat upright, I came here with Pablo. Murph insisted he didn't need to dry off, but I claimed I did. I really just wanted to talk to Pablo without Lurena around. Then Murph persuaded Lurena to ride in the boat with him. He can persuade almost anyone of almost anything.

"Let me see if I can go," Pablo says. "Wait here."

He goes out to where his mom and dad are sitting and speaks to his mom. She answers, then he returns.

"She says it's fine," Pablo says.

"What about your dad?"

"He didn't say anything, so it must be fine with him."

"It won't be fine with *my* dad. Somehow we'll have to get away without him knowing."

"Maybe Murphy can get him in the skiff, too."

"I doubt it. He's not really a skiff kind of dad."

"Neither is mine," Pablo says, peeking out the window. "He doesn't like water."

His dad is sitting in a lounge chair with a laptop. He's wearing a button-down, short-sleeve shirt; plaid shorts; and leather sandals. His hair is black, like Pablo's, and his skin is brown, too. But he reminds me more of my dad. A laptop on a camping trip. Please.

"Does your dad work in computers?" I ask.

"He's a programmer," Pablo says.

"My dad edits an online golf magazine," I say.

"We should introduce them."

"But your dad doesn't speak English, and mine doesn't speak Spanish."

"True. They could just stare at their laptops and not say anything. Like usual."

"Oh, my dad talks," I say. "He talks plenty."

Pablo laughs. As if it's funny.

"How about your mom? Does she like water?"

"Nope."

"Your sister?"

He shakes his head.

His whole family doesn't like water. I want to ask why, but it feels like it's none of my business. So I don't.

"Ready to go?" Pablo asks, standing up.

I stand up, too. "What about my clothes?"

"They won't be dry for a while. You can wear mine, if that's okay with you."

"It's okay with me if it's okay with you."

"It's okay."

"Okay," I say. "Let's go find Petopia."

18. Mosquitoitis.

That's A.G.'s latest disease. She's lying on a lounge chair by the Molloys' camper with a pained expression on her face.

In the lounge chair beside her is a girl I haven't seen before, but my guess is she's Pablo's sister. She looks like him: black hair, brown skin. She's wearing a bikini, though. And she's younger. Maybe A.G.'s age.

"Mosquitoitis," I say. "Is it serious?"

"I don't know. No Internet," A.G. says.

"Then how do you know you have it?"

"Oh, I know. I know." She coughs.

"I have it, too," the other girl says, and also coughs.

"This is my sister, Bianca," Pablo says. "She's a conformist."

"What's that?" A.G. asks.

"Someone who'll do anything to fit in."

"I think she's really sick," A.G. says.

"I am," Bianca says, and coughs again. She's getting better at it.

"I hope you two get better and have some fun," I say, then gesture to Pablo that we should keep moving.

"Don't lie around all day, Bianca," he says.

"Good-bye, Rufus," A.G. says. "Good-bye, Bianca's brother. Maybe I'll see you again! Then again, maybe not . . ."

"Good-bye, brother!" Bianca says in a sickly voice. "Bye, cute little dog!"

"It's a guinea pig, actually," I hear A.G. say as we walk away.

"I'm sure glad I don't have a little sister," I say as we walk up to my family's campsite.

"It's not so bad," Pablo says. "She copies everything I do, so we have a lot in common. It's irritating sometimes, I guess."

He guesses? That would drive me crazy.

"Pssst, Rufus!" my mom hisses. She's bent

down behind the hybrid, peeking over the hood. "Over here!"

Pablo and I run around the car and crouch down. Fido follows.

"Where's Dad?" I whisper.

"He went for a stroll."

A stroll is what my dad calls a walk.

"I unhitched the camper," Mom whispers. "Climb in. And stay down."

I open the door, and Pablo and I crawl into the backseat. Fido hops in after us. My mom gets in behind the wheel and slumps down.

"How are you going to drive like that?" I ask. "And why are we hiding if Dad isn't even around?"

"He could come back any second," she whispers.

"You can't drive like that, Mom. You'll hit a tree. Sit up."

She inches up a bit higher and pulls her seat belt across her lap. "Buckle up," she whispers.

We do. She puts the car in gear, and we ease forward.

"Oh, this is ridiculous," I say, and sit up. "It's

okay, Pablo. Sit up, Mom, and let's get out of here before—*There he is! Get down!*"

We all duck.

"Where is he?" Mom asks.

"On the trail. It's okay. His back is to us. We can go."

Mom peeks over the dashboard.

"He's heading to the bathrooms," she says. "When he's inside, we'll go."

Dad walks up to the small building and enters the door with the MEN sign above it.

"Let's go!" Mom says, and hits the gas. The tires kick up some gravel.

"Are you guys afraid of your dad or something?" Pablo asks.

Mom and I answer at the same time. She says, "No"; I say, "Yes."

19. We couldn't find the mini-mall pet paradise.

Mom says the name *Petopia* is a pun.

"They put the word *pet* with the word *utopia*," she says. "*Utopia* is a kind of paradise."

So Petopia means "pet paradise." It also means it's another one of those pet stores with a punny name.

Anyway, we can't find it.

"Sorry," Pablo says. "I was sure I saw the name on a sign."

"It's not your fault," I say, though I've been thinking for some time that he never actually saw a sign for the store at all. There aren't very many mini-malls near White Crappie Lake. We've driven pretty far and found only two little strip malls, but neither of them had a Petopia, or even a pet store.

"Maybe we came in on a different highway," he says.

I glance at Mom in the rearview mirror.

"There's only one highway that goes by the lake," she says.

Fido starts whining.

"Mom, Fido needs to go out," I say.

"Okay," she says, turning on her signal. "I should get gas anyway. Then we'll need to head back. Sorry, guys."

We nod. We're sorry, too.

She pulls off at the next exit.

Fido whines louder and hops up and down on the seat.

"I'm going to take you out as soon as Mom stops the car," I say.

I've always thought it was weird the way people speak in full sentences to their pets. Now I have one, and I do it. I know Fido can't understand English, but I do it anyway. Weird.

Mom pulls up to a bright red pump in a bright red truck stop. The huge parking lot is filled with massive eighteen-wheelers. Next to them, our hybrid seems like a toy.

Across the parking lot is a bright red convenience store the size of a supermarket. This place definitely has a bright red theme going on.

I unbuckle myself, snap Fido's leash to her collar, then open the door. She tries to bolt.

"Fido, freeze!" I say, and wrap the leash around my hand a few times. I want her close to me. She's hard to see. I don't want her getting crushed by a semi.

I climb out first and say, "Fido, heel!" She hops down onto the pavement. I check in all directions for cars, then start crossing the parking lot, scanning for a patch of grass for her to do her business in.

Pablo walks with us. "She's very obedient."

"Sometimes. But like I said, I didn't train her. Petopia—"

Right as I say the word, I see it. In neon. Bright red neon. The red neon word is written in cursive and mounted inside the store's front window.

"Look!" I say to Pablo.

He chuckles. "I knew I saw it!"

"This isn't a mini-mall, though."

"It's the size of one."

We walk up and stare at the glowing red sign. Fido barks.

"I remember we stopped here to use the bathrooms," Pablo says. "Bianca had to go."

"Whoever heard of a pet store at a truck stop?" I ask.

I look back at Mom. She's standing by the car, pumping the gas, but she's looking at us. And smiling ear to ear. She sees the sign, too.

"Go on in!" she calls. "I'll catch up!"

Fido tugs us toward the doors. Maybe she wasn't whining because she had to go out. Maybe she knew we were close. Maybe she heard other guinea pigs.

Or guinea dogs.

20. Truckers must get lonely on the wide-open road.

Driving those big rigs day after day, night after night. All alone.

The store is like a mall for truck drivers. Not only does it have shower rooms and laundry facilities, it has a game room, a food court, a gift shop, an electronics store . . . and one tiny pet shop. Fido led us right to it. There's another red neon sign hanging in its window.

I almost can't believe I'm reading it correctly. Dad searched after Petopia disappeared, and said there wasn't a pet store with that name anywhere in our whole state. And here one is, in our state, just a few miles from where we're camping, in fact. I feel an eerie chill at the back of my neck.

"I don't see any fish," Pablo says disappointedly. "But I doubt it would be a good idea for a trucker to keep an aquarium in his rig."

"I guess a snake would work better," I say, pointing at a fat boa constrictor that's hugging a branch in a terrarium.

Fido tries frantically to crawl up my pant leg, but I'm wearing shorts, so instead she crawls up my skin. Which really hurts.

"Ow!" I howl, and pry her off my leg. Just as I suspected: blood. Not enough to call 911, but still . . .

"She doesn't like snakes?" Pablo asks.

"Apparently not." I scowl at Fido, who has scurried up my shirt and now sits trembling on my shoulder. This is not exactly dog behavior.

A bird squawks. It's a blue and orange parrot resting on a perch in a cage in the corner.

"That might be a good pet for a trucker," I say. "Someone to talk to who might actually talk back."

We walk over. It has a white face with zebra stripes around its eyes.

"You think it talks?" Pablo asks.

The bird squawks again. Its tongue is gray.

"Doesn't seem to," I say.

It squawks again. This time it sounds like "No more!"

"You fellas teasing that macaw?" a deep voice asks.

It's a man wearing a bright red shirt and a name tag that says the name of the gas station and, under it, in capital letters, the word VERNE. I guess it's his name. He has gray whiskers along his jaw that turn into a beard at his chin and so many tattoos I can't make out what any of them are. His eyes are beady enough to be a little scary.

"Aw, I'm just kidding you," he says, then smiles. His eyes soften. "That's Captain Nemo. He's over thirty years old. And plenty smart. Aren't you, Nemo?"

"NEE-mo!" the bird says in its squawky voice.

So not "No more"—"Nemo."

"Like in *Twenty Thousand Leagues Under the Sea*," Pablo says.

"That's right!" Verne says. "You're plenty smart, too, boy. Have you read that book?"

"I'm reading it now, actually. Almost finished."

"That was my old man's favorite book. He named me after the author." He taps his name tag. Even his fingers have tattoos. "Verne. After . . ."

". . . Jules Verne," Pablo says. He smiles.

Verne smiles.

I'm not sure what I'm supposed to do.

"I'm afraid he's not for sale," Verne finally says. "On account of he's mine, I mean. I don't like leaving Nemo at home all day."

"NEE-mo!" the bird says.

"Maybe you want a friend for your little pal there," Verne says, sticking a finger out to Fido. Fido licks it. "He's a friendly little fella."

"She's female," Pablo says.

"Well, I'm not sure you'll want a male, then," Verne says with a laugh. "You'd have guinea pigs all over the place if you did that."

Hmm. That could solve some problems for me. . . .

"I think we do have a guinea pig around here somewhere," Verne says. "Over here . . . yeah, here it is!"

He leads us to a terrarium. There are fake plants and rocks and a little fake cave inside it, all beside a little pool of water. You'd think the terrarium would be for turtles, but inside there's a guinea pig, soaking in the water.

Verne laughs. "He's always in the water like that. Really likes being wet. Funny little fella. Does yours like being wet?"

"Actually, she does," I say.

"Rufus!" my mom says, rushing up to us. "My goodness, what a big place! Whew! I'm out of breath. Hello, there"—she peeks at Verne's name tag—"Verne." She eyes his tattoos.

"These must be your boys," Verne says. "They sure are polite."

"Well, this one's mine," Mom says, setting her hand on my head. I can't wait to grow taller. "This is his friend." She sets her hand on Pablo's shoulder.

"I see," says Verne. "Best buddies, then."

Pablo and I shrug. How embarrassing.

"So this is it," Mom says, looking around. "Petopia. It's smaller than the other one. Strange that it's in a truck stop. . . ."

"NEE-mo!" Captain Nemo squawks.

"That's my macaw," Verne says. "He's not for sale. The boys were looking at that guinea pig right there. The soggy one."

She leans in and looks at it. She smiles.

Here we go again.

21. Why does Mom think a guinea pig is the answer to everything?

We drive back to the campground with two of them, Fido and the soggy one from the terrarium. Pablo holds the new one in his lap on a beach towel Mom found in the trunk. It's a chocolate brown guinea pig with tan fur under its very whiskery chin and on its belly. Its paws are nearly black. It's been making this tiny growly, huffing sound since we left the truck stop, though every once in a while it peeps like a finch.

Fido spends the trip in my lap as well, growling at the new animal.

"I'm going to name it Snapper, after the

snapping alligator turtle Dmitri lied about," Pablo says. "Snapper kind of acted like a turtle, you know, lying in that water."

"Isn't a snapper a fish?" I ask.

"That makes it even better!"

He's acting as though the guinea pig is his when I was under the impression we'd gotten it for Murphy. I mean, what if it's a guinea dog? If it is, it's Murphy's. Period. Sure, then he'd own both a guinea dog and the world's most perfect dog, which hardly seems fair, but Murph deserves it.

"Do you know how to tell a guinea pig's sex?" Pablo asks me.

"No. But Lurena does."

"Right. The rodent expert."

Lurena will probably want the new guinea pig, too, but I don't consider her a candidate. She got Fido's pup. Plus, she already has a chinchilla and a hamster. She's got plenty of rodents. She doesn't get this one.

"So you want to hide Snapper from Dmitri, right?" Pablo asks.

Ack! This is getting as complicated as it was

when Queen Girly was born. I don't want the responsibility again of having to decide who gets the new guinea creature. Technically, since it was my mom who purchased the animal, it belongs to our family, but that doesn't make it my responsibility, does it? Why shouldn't Mom have to choose who gets it?

"It's probably a good idea," I say to Pablo. "Dmitri's going to be all over it, and when he wants something, he doesn't give up till he gets it."

"He didn't get Queen Girly. How did you get him to give up? What did you do?"

Remembering what I did makes me feel better. Less nervous.

"I said no," I say.

Pablo smiles. "So do that again."

I smile back. "You know what? I will."

Dad walks over to the car the second we drive up to the campsite. He pokes his head through the passenger-side window of the car.

"So where did you go?" he asks.

Fido barks. Dad looks into the backseat. His face falls. His shoulders, too.

"You bought another guinea pig," he says to Mom. "How on earth . . . where on earth . . . *why* on earth?"

"We found a Petopia outlet," Mom says in a chipper voice. "In a truck stop. Isn't that incredible!"

Dad looks stunned, confused, frustrated, and angry. Too stunned, confused, frustrated, and angry to find any words to yell, which, for Dad, is pretty darned stunned, confused, frustrated, and angry.

So Mom gets out of the car and walks around to his side. She takes his arm. "Have you started marinating vegetables for dinner yet?"

"N–no," he says. "I haven't had . . . Now listen, Raquel . . ."

"You'd better get started, then," she says, and starts leading him away.

"Your mom's good," Pablo says.

My mom's a lot of things. Embarrassing. Inconsiderate. Pushy. Way too chipper.

Clueless. But, yeah, Pablo's right: she's not bad. I'm particularly happy that she didn't say the guinea pig was Pablo's.

I nod. "Let's get out of here while we can."

"Where to?"

"I want to avoid Dad, Dmitri, and Lurena."

"Should we go to my RV?" Pablo asks.

If we do, it will seem as if it's his guinea pig even more than it already does.

"No, let's find Murph."

22. "Cowamundi!"

This is Dmitri saying *Coatimundi!* wrong again as he jumps off the rope swing. Murph is in the water.

"What do we do?" Pablo asks, cradling the squirming, growling guinea pig that we've wrapped inside the beach towel. The poor thing doesn't seem to like being wrapped in a beach towel, but then what guinea pig would?

"We have to get rid of Dmitri," I say.

"How?"

"You stay here behind this tree, out of sight. I'll call you when he's gone."

"What are you going to do?" Pablo asks.

"I don't know. Maybe a brilliant idea will come to me as I'm walking over there. You just keep the guinea pig hidden. Don't let it get away. I'll take Fido with me so she won't give you away."

Fido has growled and snarled and barked at the new guinea pig since we bought it. That's how she usually treats rodents: China C., Sharmet . . . Not Queen Girly, of course.

"Okay, but hurry," Pablo says. "He's sick of being wrapped up in this towel."

"I know," I say. I know I need to hurry. Pressure isn't going to help me think of a way to get rid of Dmitri.

Here are the ideas I come up with on the way over:

- I could tell him his dad has a new, expensive gadget for him.
- I could tell him I saw a wild guinea dog running through some bushes very, very far from here.
- I could tie him up with the rope swing.
- I could wait till it's his turn to jump, then, when he's underwater, grab Murph and tell him I have a surprise for him.

I decide the last one is best, though tying Dmitri up with the rope is tempting.

Unfortunately, he always lets Murph go on the swing first, then follows right after him, then climbs out of the water with him. The guy is like Murphy's shadow.

"Roof!" Murph yells from the water when he sees me.

Dmitri grumbles under his breath.

Fido runs up to Buddy and Mars, and they start tearing around in circles, Fido nipping at the bigger dogs' heels.

"Where you been?" Murph asks, swimming toward the shore. "I was looking everywhere for you. You were gone an eon."

"I was with Pablo."

"Oh, with Pablo," Dmitri says. "Guess *Doo*fus has a new best buddy."

The rope idea gets more attractive all the time.

"Come on, Roof," Murph says. "Dive in with us."

"Uh . . ." I start to glance over to where Pablo is hiding but stop myself. I don't want Murph or especially Dmitri to catch me. "Okay."

I pull off my T-shirt (technically, it's Pablo's shirt) and walk over to the rope. It's nice and strong. With a few good knots and Pablo's T-shirt for a gag, Dmitri would be out of commission for quite some time. . . .

Dmitri steps out of the water, stomps over to me, and snatches the rope out of my hand.

"Murph first!" he yells in my face, so loud I taste his lunch. Yuck.

"That's not necessary," Murph says. "Roof can go ahead of me."

Dmitri snorts like a bull. "No, you go, Murph. Then me. *Then* Rufus."

"I wouldn't think of it," Murph says, going into his proper-English-gentleman routine again. "After you, Rufus, my good man."

I get an idea.

"After *you*, Dmitri, my . . ." I can't say "my good man" to Dmitri. It's not possible. I consider saying the opposite, but instead finish my sentence by adding, "my, isn't it a beautiful day?" I try doing it with a British accent but come nowhere close.

Dmitri glares at me, then turns to Murph, who gives him a gentlemanly bow.

"Oh, all right!" Dmitri grunts, then runs backward with the rope in his hands. "Watch this, Murph—a backflip with a half turn!"

He leaps up, wraps his legs around the rope, then swings out over the water, where he releases the rope and does a feeble half back-flip, without a turn. The second he hits the water, I grab Murphy and start dragging him away.

"Hey, now!" he says. "What's all this, then?"

"I have to show you something. Come on. I don't want Dmitri to see."

"What is it, pray tell?" he asks, putting up a mild fight. "What the dickens has gotten into you, man?"

"Knock it off, Sherlock, and come on. Look, Dmitri sees us."

Dmitri is slogging through the water to the shore, bellowing, "Hey! What's up? Where you guys going?"

I answer, "Your dad got a new . . . uh . . ." That's no good. I'm stuck. I can never come up with stories on the spot.

Murphy, on the other hand . . .

"Jeepers! Your father's kayak has over-turned!" he says, pointing out at the lake. "See it? Oh, drat! It's sunk! I do hope he's all right!"

This would be a lot easier to sell without *Jeepers!* and *drat!*

Dmitri squints out to where Murph is pointing. "I don't see him."

"What's all the excitement about?" Lurena asks, walking up behind us with her cages.

Pablo is standing beside her. The beach towel is slung around his neck. I give him a fierce *where-is-it?* look. He points with his eyes at one of Lurena's cages. Sure enough, the new guinea pig is in one with Queen Girly, huffing and growling. China C. and Sharmet are sharing the other.

Fido runs over and starts growling and barking angrily at the new rodent through the bars. She doesn't like it being in there with her daughter.

"Quiet, Fido!" I say. "Sit!"

She sits and stops barking, but she continues to growl.

Fido has noticed there's a spare rodent in her daughter's cage, but neither Murphy nor Dmitri has.

"Wait! *There's* my dad!" Dmitri says, pointing to camp.

His dad is by the fire, chatting with my dad, who is marinating his vegetables.

"My bad," says Murph. "Must have been someone else tumbling out of a kayak." He claps his hands together. "Looks like dinnertime. Let's eat!"

"Yes, I hear we're having vegetable shish kebabs tonight," I say. Oh, joy.

The trick during dinner will be keeping Dad from mentioning the new rodent.

23. Most fireflies fly higher than guinea dogs.

Fido ran around the campground, snapping at them, then gagging on the few she caught and coughing them back out.

While this went on, we ate dinner. Once again, Murph saved me from my dad's insane idea of camp cuisine, this time with good old-fashioned cheeseburgers. I was able somehow to keep Dmitri away from Dad's big mouth, mostly because Dad was too busy talking about his precious shish kebabs to notice us.

I've been trying to concoct some scheme to get Dmitri out of the way so I can tell Murphy about the guinea pig. The quicker I give it to Murphy, the better. Dad can't be angry that we bought one for Murph. Dmitri will get angry at me for giving it to Murph, but he can't make much of a fuss about it. That would look like he doesn't want Murph to get the guinea pig, and he wouldn't want that.

Will Pablo be upset? Maybe, but he's got his fish, right? And he lives far away, right? So I don't have to worry about him being mad for long, right?

This will all work out beautifully, if only I can ditch Dmitri.

"So you've never been swimming?" he asks Pablo with a strong hint of mockery.

"My parents say I tried it when I was little, but I hated it."

"And his parents don't swim," I add, trying to bail him out. Maybe that's why he doesn't swim. If they never learned, they couldn't teach him. Of course, they could have gotten him lessons. . . .

"Why didn't you take swimming lessons?" Dmitri asks.

It sort of scares me when we think alike.

"They say I would always throw a really big fit—a total meltdown, yelling and screaming—

every time they put me in the water. So they stopped trying."

"Then why the heck do they take you to a *lake* for your vacation?" Dmitri asks.

Pablo shrugs. "We actually live by a lake. Lake Black Gut. So there's nothing weird about it to us. We like being near water. Not everybody who goes to a lake swims in it."

"Lake Black Gut?" I say. "Do all the lakes around here have gross names?"

"How about a game of Ghost in the Graveyard?" Lurena suggests, and gives my arm a quick tap.

Is this her idea for getting rid of Dmitri? It's worth a try.

"I'm in," I say.

"Isn't that kind of a baby game?" Dmitri says.

"I'm in," Murph says. "I like ghosts *and* babies."

Good old Murph.

"I guess I'm in," Pablo says. "Though I'm not sure what it is."

"It's simple," Lurena says. "One person is the

ghost and goes and hides. The rest of us count, 'One o'clock, two o'clock, three o'clock,' all the way to 'twelve o'clock,' then we yell, 'Starlight, star bright, I hope I see a *ghost* tonight!' Then we all go looking for the ghost. The ghost jumps out when someone comes close and tags them, which makes them the ghost, then you start over!"

Dmitri groans.

"The campfire can be base," Lurena goes on. "Who's brave enough to be the ghost first?"

Normally, Murph would jump at the chance, but this time he doesn't, which leads me to believe he knows what's up. Lurena was smart to make it sound brave to be the ghost.

"I'll do it," Dmitri says, then, looking at Pablo, he adds in a sinister tone, "And when I jump out at you, you'll be too scared to run."

"I'm scared already," Pablo says in a flat tone. "Want to feel my goose bumps?"

"I don't *think* so!" Dmitri says, sticking out his tongue.

He runs off into the woods.

"One o'clock . . . two o'clock . . . ," Lurena

starts to count, very slowly, then she whispers to me, "Show him!"

"Yeah," Murph whispers. "What's the surprise?"

Lurena gets the cage with Queen Girly and the new guinea pig in it while continuing to count out, "...four o'clock...five o'clock..." She hands the cage to me; I take it; she waves at us to leave. "...six o'clock ... seven o'clock ..."

Murph, Pablo, and I speed-walk away. Fido follows, barking at me.

"Don't worry," I whisper to her. "He won't hurt her."

"Who won't hurt who?" Murphy asks.

When we are deep in the trees, I start to open the cage. Fido starts barking louder.

"Quiet, Fido!" I order.

She stops.

"Pablo, why don't you take her to my mom and ask her to pigsit during the game? Otherwise Fido will give us away with all her barking. When Lurena finishes counting, you two should start looking for Dmitri. Take your time finding him, though."

"Okay," he says, and scoops up Fido. She starts wriggling and snarling.

"Fido, *quiet*!" I say.

She stops snarling but starts to whimper. Pablo carries her away.

That worked out well. I'm alone with Murph at last.

"So?" he says. "What's in the cage?"

I hold it up. It's dark, but the almost-half moon shines enough light for him to see what's inside.

"Hey, there are two of them!"

I quickly tell him about Petopia and buying the guinea pig.

"Does it act like a dog?" he asks eagerly.

"So far, it acts like a guinea pig. Except that it was sitting in a pool of water at the store. And it made a strange growling sound on the way home."

"Fido growls," Murph says.

"This was different. More like huffing. It hasn't obeyed any orders or begged or panted or done anything doglike yet."

"Yet," Murph says hopefully.

He reaches in and takes the guinea pig out. It starts making its weird huffing.

"Lurena says it's a boy." I say. "Pablo calls him Snapper, because he was lying in the pool of water, like a turtle. You know, the snapping-alligator-turtle thing."

Murph laughs. "It's a good name."

The guinea pig stops growling and starts squeaking and peeping.

Murph laughs again. "Listen to that! Maybe it's a guinea bird! Maybe it can fly!"

"Maybe," I say. Is it crazy that this doesn't sound crazy to me?

"Why aren't you guys looking for me?" Dmitri asks, appearing out of nowhere, mad as a monster.

The guinea pig squawks, then leaps from Murph's arms. He hits the ground, and scrambles away into the dark.

24. Who knew Fido was a bloodhound?

Not me, that's for sure.

While we all scratched our heads, trying to figure out how to find the new guinea pig, Fido put her nose to the ground and started sniffing.

"She's got the scent!" Murph says. "Follow her!"

Lurena fetches some flashlights from camp, and we're off.

"What was that anyway?" Dmitri asks. "One of Lurena's rats?"

"Nope," Lurena says. "Not one of mine."

"You were holding it, Murph." Dmitri asks, "Where did you get it from?"

No one answers. Then it hits me: we

don't have to say *where* we got it, just who it belongs to.

"It's mine," I say. "It's my new guinea pig."

"But you have Fido. What do you need another guinea pig for? It doesn't . . ." His eyes grow wide. "Does it act like a dog?"

"Not that I've noticed."

"It makes sounds like a bird," Murph says.

"A bird?" Dmitri says. "Does it . . . *fly*?"

"No, but it chirps," Murph says, and does a bird impression.

"Can we just all focus and find the rodent?" Lurena says. "There are lots of animals out here that might eat a guinea pig. Raccoons, for instance. And coyotes."

"Are there coyotes out here?" Dmitri asks.

I think he might be scared.

"Are you scared, Dmitri?" Lurena asks, smiling at him.

Oh, no. Now I'm thinking like her, too.

"No!" he says. "I just don't know why we're out here looking for a stupid guinea pig with coyotes around. Obviously, we'll never find it. I'm heading back." He starts doing that.

Lurena laughs. "Coyotes won't bother us. At least, not if we all stay together. They might attack a kid out in the woods by himself, though."

Dmitri stops walking. "Why didn't you tell me about that before, when I went off to hide for your dumb game?"

Fido keeps searching, sniffing the ground, stopping sometimes, like she's lost the scent, then barking and moving on again.

"Do you think she can find him?" Pablo asks.

"Of course she can!" Murph replies in a big, confident voice. "She's Fido the guinea dog!"

"Guinea bloodhound," I say.

"Exactly!" Murph says, and slaps me on the back.

"This is stupid," Dmitri says.

"You still here?" I ask.

"I'm going back," he says.

"See you, coyote chow," Lurena says.

I wish she'd stop that coyote stuff and let him leave.

"Ha-ha," Dmitri says, without laughing. "Coming with, Murph?"

Murph and Lurena crack up in unison.

"Fine. I'll go by myself. You're not going to find a guinea pig out here in the dark, I'll tell you that. You'll come back with nothing." And he walks off, the beam of his flashlight wobbling. He's scared, all right.

"Are there really coyotes out here?" Pablo asks.

"I hope so," Lurena says.

Fido leads us out of the trees to the lake. She sniffs the ground right up to the bank, then skids to a stop. She sniffs a moment at the air, which is dotted with fireflies—she doesn't eat any, not while she's working—then she barks out at the lake.

We all walk up to the bank and look down into the dark water.

"Think Snapper dove in?" Pablo asks. His voice trembles, like he's worried. I think he's gotten attached. Darn it.

"Guinea pigs don't generally dive into water," Lurena says.

"Except Fido," Murph says.

"And Snapper," Pablo says. "He was in water when we first saw him."

"At Petopia," Lurena says. "If that's where you got him, there's no telling what he'll do."

"What if he can't swim?" Pablo asks.

"Maybe he's a guinea turtle and can swim beautifully," Murph says.

"But he doesn't have a shell. What if something gets him? What if Dmitri's right and there really is an alligator snapping turtle?"

"There isn't," I say, though I was wondering the same thing myself.

"Can't you guys dive in after him, see if you can find him?" Pablo asks.

"It's too dark," Lurena says. "It'd be impossible. Even Fido didn't dive in. We'll have to wait till morning."

We all stand quietly awhile, staring at the quiet lake. The rope swing is far to our left. We've covered some ground. The moonlight flickering on the water's surface reminds me of the fireflies hovering around our heads.

If I weren't so worried, I'd probably be enjoying this.

I crouch down and pet Fido. "Good girl," I say. "Good girl."

She pants. She likes strokes.

I remember when Fido ran away. I was tired of all the attention I was getting for having a guinea dog and tried to train the dog out of her. Then she disappeared. She was gone all night. I was so scared something would happen to her outside in the dark.

"You think he's okay out there?" I ask Fido.

She yaps, and her little voice echoes across the lake.

"I'll take that for a yes."

25. Guinea turtle?

Guinea bird?

Or just a chirping amphibian guinea pig?

Whatever Snapper is, we're looking for him, in Murph's skiff. Murph, Lurena, and me. It's pretty crowded, but one of us convinced the other two she was "essential to the expedition," being an "authority on rodent behavior." Murph invited her aboard with his usual the-more-the-merrier nonsense.

Pablo stayed ashore.

Fido, our guinea bloodhound, is with us, too, of course. She's perched on the bow. Maybe she's a guinea bird dog that hunts guinea birds.

I'm probably pushing this "guinea" thing too far.

What does *guinea* mean anyway? And

why are guinea pigs called *guinea pigs* when they're obviously rodents? Why not *guinea rats*?

There's a person in this boat who can answer these questions, but I'm not going to ask her. I don't want to waste precious time listening to her rattle off guinea facts.

Not that anyone needs to ask her to rattle off guinea facts.

"Guinea pigs do like water," she says. "Most rodents can swim."

"Yeah, just look at all of them," I say, spreading my arms. "White Crappie Lake is practically a rodent swimming pool."

"I didn't say they *love* to swim. I said that they *can* swim, if they need to. But there are aquatic rodents, you know. Beavers, for example. Definitely rodent. Look at their teeth."

"Where?" Murph says, twisting his head side to side exaggeratedly.

Lurena laughs. "You know what I mean, Murphy Molloy, you big goof."

Fido suddenly scoots to the port side of the boat; she whimpers and wags her bottom.

"I think she smells something," I say, and point off to the left. "That way."

"Right oar, oarsman," Murph says in an Irish or maybe Scottish accent. He rolls the *r* in *right* and *oarsman*. "Rrrow, rrrow, rrrow yerrr boat!"

"Okay," I say. "We're rowing already."

"Gently down the strrrrrream! Merrrrrrrrily, merrrrr—"

"Enough!" I say, though I'm laughing. "We're going in a circle." I try to roll the *r* in *circle*, but can't. I bet Pablo can.

"Oarrrrsman, left oarrr! Rrrow, rrrow! . . ."

"That fixed it," I interrupt. "We're good."

Fido leads us toward some cattails.

"Oarrrs up!" Murph calls.

"I'm right here, you know," I say. "You don't have to yell."

"Sorrrry," he says.

The skiff cruises into the reeds. They graze against the sides of the boat, slowing it down.

Fido barks and barks.

"I think we're close," Lurena says.

"Cowamundi!" yells Dmitri. He's in his kayak. He must have been hiding in the reeds.

He's paddling toward us from starboard. Not fast, since it's hard to paddle through cattails, but fast enough that we can't get out of the way.

"Are you crazy?" Lurena screams.

He laughs like the villain he is as his kayak crashes into the skiff. We all fall to the left.

"Midsea collision!" Murph yells. "Pull the alarrrm! Man the lifeboats!"

I scowl at him. Doesn't he ever just get mad? Is everything fun and games to this guy?

"Where's Fido?" Lurena gasps.

I spin around, looking for her. She isn't on board.

"Dog overrrboard! Dog overrrboard!" Murph hollers.

Fido can swim, of course, so I'm not too worried. But can she swim in these reeds? And I'd be lying if I said I wasn't worried about that mythical alligator snapping turtle, or some other carnivorous creature—one of Lurena's aquatic rodents, maybe—prowling the cattails.

"There she is!" Murph says.

I follow where he's pointing. She's swimming away from, instead of toward, the boat.

"Fido!" I call. "Come *here*, girl! This way! *Come!*"

She glances back but keeps swimming away. She wants us to follow her.

"Oarsmen," I say, "full speed ahead!"

26. Empty speed ahead.

Is that the opposite of *full speed ahead*? Oars are too long to work in cattails. Rowing is impossible. So Murph and I lean over the side and paddle with our hands.

"You guys all right?" a voice calls from the shore. It's Pablo. He must have run all the way around.

"We're fine!" Lurena calls back.

She would say that. She's not up to her elbows in scummy muck. The water's a lot muddier in the reeds.

"Dmitri rammed us with his kayak," I say to Pablo. Where'd Dmitri go anyway? I don't see him anywhere.

I do see Pablo, through the cattails. He's pacing.

"Did you find Snapper?" he asks.

"Not yet," Lurena answers. "But Fido's on his trail."

Much to our surprise, Pablo answers, "I'm coming in!"

Coming in?

I see him step toward the bank.

"Not a good idea," I say. "The bottom here is thick mud. It's slippery and deep."

He stops. "Well, I can't just stand here!"

"If we can get to you, will you get into the boat?" I ask.

He doesn't answer.

"Pablo?"

"I guess so," he says.

Murph looks at me and smiles. I know what he's thinking: he's proud of Pablo. Happy for him. I am, too.

"Let's go get him," I say to Murph.

"I don't think we have room, Roof."

"I'll jump out when we pick him up," Lurena says. "Pablo getting into a boat is worth losing your rodent expert."

"Right," I say. I'm surprised she volunteered,

considering the fancy clothes she's wearing.

"Fido's swimming along the shore," I say to Pablo. "Be ready in case we get close enough for you to climb in. If Fido changes direction, though, we're going to follow her."

"Okay," he says. He sounds shaky. I'm sure he's nervous about going out in the boat.

We keep trailing Fido as she leads us through the cattails. Murph and I start grabbing the reeds and pulling the boat through them. It works better than rowing.

We're moving parallel to the bank, so we can't get close enough to pick up Pablo. He walks along the shore, following us, just in case we find a way to get to him. He's going to a lot of trouble for the new guinea pig. He really has gotten attached.

The cattails start to thin out a little, making it easier for us to get through. Fido's still ahead, paddling like crazy. She never seems to tire. We drift into a small clearing.

"There he is!" Murph says. "There's Snapper!"

I guess that's the name. No sense fighting it.

Snapper is floating on his back about twenty or so feet ahead of us. He has something in his paws. It's flapping around . . .

"I think he has a . . . ," Lurena says, then lowers her voice. "A *fish*!"

"What does he have?" Pablo asks.

I guess that's why Lurena whispered. Snapper has caught a fish, and Pablo loves fish. I wonder if the fish is a white crappie. Or maybe a snapper . . . ?

"You know what he reminds me of?" Lurena whispers. "Swimming on his back with a fish on its chest?"

Before she can tell me, Snapper disappears under the water. He didn't twist and dive in. It was as if he was surprised to be going under, as if he didn't mean to do it. In fact, he made a little squawk before he slipped beneath the surface. It was almost as if something had pulled him under.

27. Heroic, sure, but not smart.

That's what Pablo diving into the pond to save his guinea pig is. It's also surprising, considering how he feels about water. Any one of us could have done it, and we're all fine with water. But Pablo dives in anyway. It's a clumsy dive, but it's his first one ever, so . . . Throw in the possibility that there's something under the water that snatches guinea pigs—a snapping turtle?—and you've got one heroic, foolish, surprising, clumsy, death-defying dive. I love it. If I were a judge, I'd hold up a scorecard with a big ten on it.

Of course, Murph and I do have to jump in to save him. I mean, the kid doesn't know how to swim.

The bottom of the pond is so deep with oozy mud that I can't stand up. I sink in up to my ankles. It's kind of creepy, like I'm being dragged under by a cold alien slime.

"Tread water," Murph says. "The bottom's too muddy."

I lean forward into the water and swim. My feet pull free from the slime and I start paddling. Murph and I swim over to Pablo. I grab hold of one flailing arm; Murph gets the other. Together, we keep Pablo's head up out of the water. Fido swims in a circle around us, barking.

"Snapper!" Pablo screams when he's not coughing up lake water. "Snapper!"

"We'll find him, Pablo!" Lurena yells from the skiff. "Let them save *you* first!"

His struggling makes it twice as difficult to get him into the boat. A couple of times, he almost tips it over. When we finally push him in, Murph taps my shoulder.

"Let's stay in the water. We can pull the boat out of the reeds."

"How?" I ask.

He grabs hold of the mooring line.

"Like tugboats."

He swims ahead, gripping the rope. I take the other line and do as he does. The boat glides behind us. Fido paddles ahead of us.

"Any sign of Snapper, Lurena?" Murph yells out.

"No. Do you think the snapping turtle got him?"

"There's no snapping turtle," Pablo says.

"I know you don't want to hear it, Pablo," Lurena says, "but something took your little friend. It was terribly brave of you to dive in to save him, though, especially with your being afraid of the water and all."

"I never said I was afraid of it," he says. "I said I didn't like it. I've been in it plenty of times. I wish you all would hear me on this."

When we clear the reeds, I see behind us, floating in the cattails—*hidden* in the cattails—Dmitri's kayak. He's not in it.

I tap Murph's shoulder. "Look," I whisper, pointing at the kayak.

He nods. "Let's get in."

"Check," I say.

My dad doesn't like it when I say that. Murph doesn't mind.

We climb aboard the skiff. It's crowded inside. And heavy. It sinks deeper into the water.

"I think we're carrying one too many," Murph says. "How about one of us rides in Dmitri's kayak?"

"Huh?" Pablo and Lurena say.

I point, and they look at where the kayak is drifting, unmanned. It's not sitting still, though. It keeps rocking. As we get closer, I can see why. A hand is holding on to it. Dmitri's hand. He's in the water on the other side of it. He probably couldn't get back in after he swam over, swiped Snapper, then swam back, the whole time underwater. I wonder where Snapper is now. Is he in the kayak? Did he get away?

Fido starts barking.

"Someone over there, girl?" Murph asks.

"Is it Snapper?" Pablo asks, and stands up.

The boat rocks dangerously.

"Sit down, please, sailor, or we'll all end up in the drink," Murph says.

Pablo sits.

Dmitri's kayak suddenly rolls over on its side.

Fido barks louder and looks down at the water. A small, black-colored animal surfaces near the tipped kayak, then immediately submerges again, all in one motion, like a whale, only smaller.

A few feet ahead, it does it again. Is it an otter?

"It's Snapper!" Lurena yells.

Fido dives in after him.

Then Pablo does.

We're back where we started.

28. Dog-paddling isn't just for dogs.

Pablo figures it out pretty quickly. Or did he already know how? He is swallowing a fair amount of water, especially when he calls out, "Here, boy! Here, Snapper!"

What is he, crazy? Does he think Snapper's a guinea dog? It seems more like he's the proud owner of a guinea *otter*. I guess it's a good thing Pablo lives on a lake.

Lurena tries rowing the boat around us, to head Snapper off, I suppose, but instead she almost takes *my* head off with one of her oars.

"Hey!" I splutter. "Oarswoman! Oars down! Oars down!"

"Sorry," she yells back. "Just trying to help!"

"Just don't!"

With Pablo keeping himself afloat and Lurena not swiping at us with wooden blades, Murph and I are free to swim ahead and try to corral Snapper. All we have to do is follow Fido. She never gives up. Like any good dog, she is steadfast.

We chase Snapper to the bank. He scrambles up onto it, stops for a second to shake off some water, then starts running in that funny, loping—yep, otterish—way of his. Fido follows him up the bank, likewise shakes off water, then shoots after him. Being faster, she overtakes him easily and tackles him. They snarl and growl and roll around together in the grass. I think they're playing. I hope they are.

I swim over to the bank and climb up onto it. Murph stays in the water to help Pablo. Since I don't have a fur coat, I don't shake off the water. I run over to the battling rodents. I'm hesitant at first to stick my hands in between the snarling, tangling fighters, then I remember they're guinea pigs, and I reach in and pick them up by their soggy scruffs.

"Okay, that was fun," I say. "Good girl, Fido."

She pants proudly.

Behind me I hear a loud thump. It's the sound of wood hitting fiberglass. Lurena has rammed the skiff into Dmitri's kayak.

"Are you crazy?" Dmitri yells. I can't see him. He's still hiding behind the kayak, which is now upside down on the water. "You'll break it! My dad will kill me!"

"I didn't mean to do it, you big dope," Lurena says. "I'm trying to rescue you. Give me your hand."

"I'm not holding your hand!" he says.

"Fine," she says. "Rescue yourself."

She starts to row away.

"Okay, okay," Dmitri says. "Lower a paddle, and I'll grab it."

"It's an oar, not a paddle," she says, and lowers one.

Murph and Pablo catch up to me.

"Snapper!" Pablo sighs. "Come here, boy!"

I hand him the guinea pig. It's crystal clear that Snapper belongs to Pablo. Murphy's smile shows me he knows it, too.

Lurena starts towing Dmitri and his kayak to shore.

I get an idea.

"Tell Dmitri I had to . . . ," I start to say to Murph, then get stuck coming up with an excuse. Why is this so hard for me? "Tell him I...I...I had to go to the bathroom? Yeah. That's fine. Then tell him to be careful because there have been snapping turtle sightings here." I wink.

"Gotcha," he says.

"For the last time, there are no snapping turtles here," I hear Pablo say as I run off, toward the cattails. I'm sure Murph will clue him in.

I step into the water, into the mud, and slowly my feet sink in. It's not as oozy close to the bank. I work my way over to the reeds, crouch down in them as low as I can, and wait.

As Lurena and Dmitri near the shore, Murph says, "You should be careful. There have been snapping turtle sightings around here."

Pablo nods. "Yeah," he says.

"Oh, really?" Dmitri says with a little laugh. He climbs out of the boat and steps into the water. "I guess I'd better watch out."

I swim toward him, underwater, and seize his ankle with a viselike grip.

He screams and starts jumping around. He accidentally kicks me in the head, trying to get away. I let go and surface. My ears are ringing, but it was totally worth it.

Murph and Pablo are cracking up. Fido is barking at Dmitri.

"Don't be grabbing me, dude!" he says.

"Don't be stealing other people's pets, *dude*."

"Don't tell me what to do!"

"You knocked Fido into the water!" I'm getting angry.

"She can swim all right. No harm done."

"What about Murph's boat? You rammed it!"

He looks up at Murph. "Sorry about that, Murph. It was an accident."

"Tell it to the police," Lurena says.

Dmitri glares at her. "So whose guinea pig is that? It's a cool swimmer."

"It's Pablo's," I say. "I bought him at Petopia, and I gave him to Pablo."

"Petopia?" Dmitri asks. "What are you talking about? There's no Petopia around here." He's practically foaming at the mouth.

"It was in a truck stop," Pablo says.

"But I bet it isn't there now," I add.

"Liar," he says. "You didn't get that guinea pig at Petopia. You're lying because you don't want me to have one. But if you bought it at a truck stop, I'll find it."

"They only had one guinea dog, and we bought it," Pablo says.

"You shut up, weirdo," Dmitri says, pointing at Pablo.

We all stand there a minute, his meanness filling the air.

Then he hoists himself up onto the bank, climbs into his kayak, and paddles away.

"You know," Murph says, "sometimes the *less* the merrier."

Whoa. Did I really hear that from Murphy Molloy? Forget the guinea pig acting like an otter. This is the true miracle.

29. The guinea dog chased the guinea squirrel up a tree.

The strangest thing about this is that the squirrel is the dog's daughter.

As she scampers along a high branch that reaches out over the lake, Lurena shouts, "Queen Girlisaurus! Get back here!"

Fido runs under the branch to the water's edge, then looks up and barks at her daughter. She's being scolded by two moms.

Lurena flicks an angry look at me. "Do you see? Do you see why I keep her in her cage?"

"No," I say. "I see that she's glad you finally let her out. You can't keep a squirrel in a cage. You have to let her run and climb."

Lurena sets her fists on her hips. She

frowns. Then her mouth twists so that it's like she's half frowning and half smiling.

"I guess you're right," she says. "But you just better hope a raccoon doesn't get her."

"Or a snapping turtle," Murph says.

"Right!" Pablo laughs.

Snapper runs below Queen Girly, on the ground. He heads for the water's edge, then dives in and starts swimming, otter-style, under the branch. He stops when he's under Girly, then rolls onto his back and floats.

I guess I should find all this really bizarre. But I don't. I'm getting used to guinea pigs not acting like guinea pigs. I'm pretty sure I know now why they don't act like the animals they are. They came from Petopia—or, in Queen Girly's case, from an animal that came from Petopia.

I don't find it strange anymore that the store turned up in the truck stop, or that it had just the pet Pablo needed, just when he needed it. It's not strange that it was there for my mom the night she bought Fido, the perfect guinea pig for a kid who wanted a dog but couldn't get one, or that Fido gave birth to the exact animal Lurena wanted but her parents wouldn't let her have. Guinea pigs that can catch a Frisbee, or climb a tree, or swim underwater? Strange, sure, but it makes sense that they act that way. Petopia is in the business of sensible strangeness.

My guess is the store appears when and where it's needed, then, once it delivers the strange but perfect pet to the lucky new pet owner, it vanishes. Maybe it goes to some other place, some other town, or state, or country, where some other kid needs some other peculiarly perfect pet. Maybe this happens over and over, all around the world.

This time, it showed up for Pablo in a truck stop near White Crappie Lake. Maybe, at this moment, it's reappearing in some faraway place: in a shopping mall in Chicago, or in an airport in Japan, or next to a souvenir shop near the Great Pyramids of Egypt. For all I know, some kid is walking into a Petopia in Africa right this minute and buying a guinea pig that acts like a gorilla, or a kid in Australia is buying a guinea pig that acts like a kangaroo. Who knows, maybe it isn't just guinea pigs. I mean, the truck-stop Petopia had other animals: the boa constrictor, for example, and Captain Nemo. I wonder what he acts like when you get him home. . . .

"Oh!" Lurena shrieks. "Look!"

Queen Girly has gone out to the end of the branch, onto tinier branches of the branch, one of which has cracked under her tiny weight. She's hanging on by a paw; her other three grasp frantically at the air.

Fido goes bonkers. She dives into the water, which frightens Snapper, who chirps and dives under. Buddy then goes bounding down and runs into the lake. (Mars doesn't, because he's with Dmitri and his dad in their SUV, out looking for Petopia. My bet is they won't find it.)

So the strange gets stranger. The guinea squirrel hanging from the limb; the guinea dog and the perfect dog swimming in circles below, barking, one in a deep voice, one in a tiny one; and the guinea otter, surfacing in the nearby reeds, on its back, with a fish in its paws.

"Snapper eats fish," Murphy says, looking at Pablo. "That okay with you?"

Pablo shrugs. "I eat fish."

"Ah," Murph says. "Then all is well."

30. Man eats dog.

A hot dog, that is, and the man, incredibly, is Dad.

"Admit you like it," Mom says.

The adults all laugh.

Dad hesitates, looks down at the remainder of the hot dog in his hand—it's smeared with ketchup, mustard, and pickle relish—then he laughs, too, and stuffs the whole thing into his mouth.

Miracles happen at White Crappie Lake.

A moment later, though, Dad gags on the enormous bite he took, covers his mouth with his hand, and keeps the dog inside—something Dmitri had not been able to do. Of course, Dmitri had eaten five. This is Dad's first.

The guy has really loosened up some on this

trip. All the parents, in fact, are acting pretty chummy. Campfires have that effect on people. Even Austin hangs around the fire at night instead of hibernating with his video games.

The only problem is that being around laughing, joking adults is way less fun than it sounds. When they're happy and relaxed, they're more likely to loudly relate some embarrassing moment from your childhood, or to start singing some song you used to sing, then beg you to join in.

"Let's get out of here," I whisper to Murph.

He looks at me like I'm crazy. "Why? It's merry here!"

I bet he'd love hearing his mom telling an embarrassing episode from his childhood. He'd even get up and reenact it for everyone. He'd happily sing any song he's ever known, including "Baby Beluga" or "Little Bunny Foo Foo." He'd happily belt it out.

Let him. I don't like singing. I'm leaving.

"Ghost in the Graveyard?" he asks. "Is that it?"

"Yes, that's it precisely," I say, though I wasn't

thinking of the game. I was only thinking of getting away. "Let's go play Ghost in the Graveyard. Just shut your mouth and come on . . ."

"Wait, we need people to play!" He jumps up on a stump. "Ladies and gentlemen? I beg your pardon! Quiet, please!"

Oh, help.

"Tonight we have some festivities planned. A rousing match of Ghost in the Graveyard! But we will need participants. Who will play?"

He makes a broad gesture with his arms, as if he's gathering everyone up. The more the merrier. The more the scarier, more like. I don't want to play tag with Lurena's parents. It's bad enough playing with her. Will I have to tag Lurena's dad? Or *mine*?

Several of the adults say, "I will!" and raise their hands, laughing like idiots. Then they nudge the ones who didn't volunteer, and say, "Oh, come on, wet blanket!" or "Don't be a killjoy!" Where do adults learn to talk?

Lurena and Pablo are sitting at the picnic table, peeking into Lurena's cages. Snapper

161

is in one with Queen Girly (who survived her climbing misadventure by dropping into the water and being rescued by her mother—Fido, that is). If Pablo didn't put Snapper in the cage, he'd jump in the lake, and, though Pablo now goes in the water, he doesn't exactly like to. Not to mention it's dark out, and dinnertime. It's reasonable Pablo would want to keep the guinea otter on dry land.

Before you know it, everyone's playing the game, including Pablo's parents, Austin, even A.G. and Bianca. Their mosquitoitis must be better. Only Dmitri's mom absolutely refuses to play. She has a headache, she says, and retreats to the Sulls' RV.

Maybe I should have a headache.

Murphy, of course, is the first ghost. Everyone runs off to hide, giggling and whispering and tripping off into the dark.

I see Pablo climbing a tree and remember that he was in a tree the first time I saw him, when he gave me the advice that saved Fido from choking to death. I'm sure glad I met him. He says he'll tell his parents he wants to coordinate our summer trips so we're at White Crappie at the same time from now on. And he gave me his e-mail address so we can talk all year round.

I hide, too, but I don't giggle or whisper or trip. I swipe a hot dog and a bun, and sneak under the picnic table to eat it. Fido finds me. She jumps up in my lap and starts licking my chin. It could be love, but it's probably the wienie.

"Down!" I command in a whisper.

She gets down and whimpers.

"Quiet!" I whisper-command.

She stops whimpering.

"Good girl." I pat her head. She pants. I break a piece off my hot dog and feed it to her.

Murphy ducks his head under the table. "I s-e-e-e-e you!" he says in a ghostly voice.

"I'm kind of comfortable under here," I say. "Why don't you go find someone else to tag, then come back?"

"Check," he says in his regular, nonghostly voice, and runs away.

I take another bite of my hot dog and feed

another bite to my guinea dog. We watch the fire flicker as we chew.

"It was a fun trip," I say to her. "I didn't think it would be."

She looks me straight in the eye as I talk. I know she doesn't understand English, but I swear she understands me.

Murph returns, out of breath, and climbs in under the table with us. He swiped a hot dog, too. He even took the time to squirt some ketchup on it. I'm jealous. Mine's already gone. And it didn't have ketchup.

"Here, take half," he says, and breaks his dog in two.

"Thanks," I say, and take my half. We both take a bite.

"I'm sorry you didn't get Snapper," I say.

He shrugs, like, *Hey, no biggie.*

And that's all we need to say about it.

"Did you know that the first hot dog wasn't made of pork or beef?" he says through his hot dog.

"No," I say through mine.

"You'll never guess what it was made of."

164

"You're probably right."

"You're not going to guess?"

"You're not going to tell me?"

He laughs. "Cat! They were actually called *hot cats*."

Fido growls.

I give her another piece of meat.

"No wonder she likes it," I say.

Murph laughs again, harder. I love making him laugh.

"So I ride home with you, right?" I ask.

"Yep," he says.

"You checked with your parents?"

"I don't need to. They will love having you."

"You sure?"

"*Paws*itive."

"Can I tell you something about Petopia?"

"*Paws*itively."

"Okay, it was cute once . . ."

"Sorry." He fake-hangs his head in shame.

"So I can tell you?"

"Shoot."

"I think . . . well . . . the animals they sell . . . I think . . ." I stop. It sounds too crazy.

He lifts his head. "I agree," he says.

"About what? I mean . . . you *do*?"

"*Paws*iti—Oops. Sorry." He hangs his head again.

"I bet we'll find another Petopia," I say. "We'll get you a guinea something yet."

"Don't worry about it," he says, looking up. "I got Buddy. I got you. I got Fido. What else do I need?"

Good old Murph.

"Another hot dog?" I ask.

"Two, coming right up."

"With ketchup, please," I say. "And yellow mustard. Not brown."

"Is there any other way?"

He bangs me with his shoulder. I bang him back: 2 guys + 2 dogs + ketchup = fun × 100 trillion.

"I found you!" Lurena yells, sticking her head under the table.

I feel too good to let her spoil the fun. Maybe we can add one crazy girl to this equation.

"We're kind of comfortable under here," I say. "Go find someone else to tag, then get three hot dogs with ketchup and come back."

"I'm vegetarian," she says.

"So get a tofu dog from my dad."

"Check," she says. She's picking up my lingo.

Fido barks, then paws at my knee.

"Oh, and get a dog for the guinea dog," I say.

"Be right back with your order," Lurena says. "You need anything else with that? Fries? S'mores?"

"No," I say. "We have everything we need."

Patrick Jennings

is the author of many popular novels for middle-schoolers, including *Guinea Dog, Lucky Cap, Invasion of the Dognappers, We Can't All Be Rattlesnakes,* and *Faith and the Electric Dogs.* He won the 2013 Kansas William Allen White Children's Book Award and the 2011 Washington State Scandiuzzi Children's Book Award for *Guinea Dog,* which was also a 2013 Honor Book for the Massachusetts Children's Book Award. In addition it was nominated for the 2010-2011 New Hampshire Great Stone Face Book Award, the 2011-2012 Colorado Children's Book Award, the 2012-2013 Florida Sunshine State Young Reader's Award, the 2014 Washington State Sasquatch Award, the 2014 Hawaii Nēnē Award, the 2014-2015 Indiana Young Hoosier Book Award, and the 2014-2015 Minnesota Maud Hart Lovelace Book Award. He lives in a small seaport town in Washington State.

You can visit him online at www.patrickjennings.com.